the perfect girl

*What happens
when you get
everything you want—
and it isn't enough?*

barb huff

BARBOUR
PUBLISHING

ISBN 1-58660-980-7

Published by Barbour Publishing, Inc., P.O. Box 719, Uhrichsville, Ohio 44683, www.barbourbooks.com

Our mission is to publish and distribute inspirational products offering exceptional value and biblical encouragement to the masses.

Member of the
Evangelical Christian
Publishers Association

Printed in the United States of America.

5 4 3 2 1

dedication

For Chrissy Shafer and the Jacko for all your help
finding the characters in these stories.
I love you guys.

Also, to all "my kids,"
past, present, and future.
May you see the gifts and talents
God has given each of you
and may you use them for His Glory.

To Raina ~
I hope you enjoy
this book and the
wisdom it holds.
Love,
Aunt Susan
5/5/04

about the author

Barb Huff is the former director of youth and family programs. She has published devotionals on parenting and teen nonfiction articles in *Guideposts for Teens, Group,* and other publications. She lives in north-eastern Ohio with her husband, son, and foster children.

E very anticipated memory for the coming months fizzled like an old match the minute Jenna Rose Brinley opened her mouth and that first note sprang forth. A glimmer brighter than the gold tones behind the pulpit appeared in the pastor's eyes, and the youth pastor could hardly contain his glee as he bit his lip. For a brief moment, even Cheryl, the organist, paused and scanned the crowd for the melodic source. One by one, members of the congregation faded away until the only voice left was that of the fifteen-year-old with the blond locks of hair wisping around her shoulders.

"Who's that?" Andria whispered to her twin sister as she surveyed the new face across from them. The girl, all alone in the second pew, continued with her song as if every voice was still in sync with hers.

Darby gave a fleeting glance, pencil in hand, and continued with the rosebud she was sketching on the back of the bulletin. "No idea." She tucked a lock of dusty brown hair behind an ear with her free hand. "Whoever she is, she can sing, that's for sure."

"Doesn't she realize like no one else is singing?" Andria mumbled as she glanced around the sanctuary. Pairs of eyes from all angles of the room were fixed on the young guest.

"I would say chances are she likes it that way."

The younger of the fourteen-year-old twins nodded slowly and studied the newcomer as she continued with the words of the hymn. In her hands, the blond held only a pink, fuzzy-covered Bible with a clunky blue fish zipper pulley.

Spend your entire life in the same church, singing the same songs, and still don't know the words, and then along comes this person, and she knows them word for word.

The girl's dress was a simple powder blue tank dress—the color made her hair shine in the sunlight. The poise with which she sang and the way her eyes closed ever so slightly as she hit the high notes without a quiver led Andria to quickly agree with her sister. Darby was right. Not only did she probably like it that way, she probably *wanted* it that way.

"Maybe she's just visiting," she said out loud to herself. Her sister, engrossed in her latest sketches, once again just shrugged. The knot in Andria's stomach seemed to tell her otherwise.

This girl wasn't leaving anytime soon.

A smile spread across Jenna Rose Brinley's face as her eyes fell on the title of the hymn about to be sung. She couldn't have scripted it better herself. There's nothing like an entrance to get noticed, and, well, belting out the song that she had just performed as a solo at her home church days before should do the trick quite well.

When her father told her that he was discussing taking the associate pastor's position at Faith Calvary Temple, Jenna Rose was furious. She was about to enter her freshman year—which meant homecoming courts, varsity dance squad, and, most importantly, one of the best women's choirs in the state. There was no reason that he needed to uproot them and move to the middle of Ohio, of all places in the world. Life was good. Starting all over again was not in her immediate plans.

But, like usual, he did as he pleased without discussing things with her first.

From his seat across from the pulpit, her father caught her eye. He looked small sitting there in his dark blue double-breasted suit against the purple hues all around the sanctuary, his hair parted and brushed stiffly against his head. His frame looked lost in the heavily carved, high-backed chair. There was a lot of purple here in this room, she realized as she looked around. He smiled and nodded as if to say, "Memorize that shade, sweetie, because we need to go find me a tie to go with it." Too bad she wasn't telepathic—she would suggest that a Barney the Dinosaur suit would be just about as easy to find as that hideous shade for a tie—except maybe in a clown shop. Something told her that he would find the suggestion less than amusing. File the Barney reference away for a conversation with Amy. Her best friend would get it—even if she were hundreds of miles away.

As the pianist started the song, a twinkle seemed to rest in Carl Brinley's eyes. She loved that glimmer. It was a spark that was saved for only his daughter at her finest moments. Unfortunately, it didn't show itself that often. Most of the time, he was too busy to care. This time, he seemed to know as well as she did that his one and only baby girl was about to make her entrance.

Her voice rose strong above the reserved congregation.

Even Jenna Rose was caught with surprise as the voices began to trail off. By the second verse, she was going it alone. Her eyes were closed as usual when she sang, but she could feel their stares all around her. Her voice fed off their silence—others may say that the audience's adulation makes their performance better—not Jenna Rose. Awe and silence meant they were spellbound. And spellbound was the way she liked to leave them.

The last chords of the piano wafted through the sanctuary as she dutifully lowered her chin in prayer stance. Fighting back a smile, she cleared her throat and clutched her Bible close to her chest.

Jenna Rose Brinley had arrived.

CHAPTER 22

I swear if I have to hug another blue hair who smells like old Avon perfume, I am going to ralph," Jenna Rose complained into her cell phone as she pulled the car door closed behind her. A comfortable laugh came through the receiver. It was nice to hear Amy's voice as if she were right there walking out of church with her. The sound was familiar and comfortable—not like everything here. Jenna Rose closed her eyes, remembering the thousands of times they had fled the hugs and cheek-pinching at her old church together. They would find refuge under the back stairs and discuss the latest gossip until they decided they wanted to be found. Would she ever have that again? Man, she missed Amy. She kicked her shoes off, pulled her knees up to her chest, and adjusted her dress to cover them. "I'm probably going to have to sit here in the car forever now. He's still nowhere to be seen."

"Your house isn't close to the church?" Amy asked.

"Of course not. We're like clear on the other side of town." She turned the auxiliary switch in the car and flipped on the radio. "Not like this town is that big or anything. I could walk it. If I was desperate enough."

"Look on the bright side. I heard that in Ohio you can get your permit at like fifteen and a half or something. So just a little over a month and you can be on your own. Then you can come get me, and we'll terrorize that new town together."

Jenna Rose chuckled sarcastically. "Oh yeah. Like that's going to happen with my dad. He'll never let me drive. And if he does, I'm sure I'll be thirty before I'll be allowed to go to Georgia by myself. What is this?" Country music poured out of the speakers at every stop of the seek controls. "I swear I have moved to Hicksville, USA. If it's not country, then it's eighties' music. And I just left Savannah, you know. Please! Country music everywhere, but you could at least find a little hip-hop once in awhile or something."

"I happen to like eighties' music," her friend piped in.

"Yeah, but you don't listen to it on purpose!" Plopping her head against the back of the car seat, she sighed loudly. Amy could be such a dork at times. She would say anything just for the sake of an argument. "I mean, these people have whole channels devoted to eighties' stuff, like it's 1984 all over again or something. I bet they don't even know who Britney is around here."

"Like you could be so lucky," Amy replied with a laugh.

"Please. She's better than Wang Chung, thank you very much."

"Says you. Well, I hate to go, Jenna, but my dad is givin' me the evil eye."

With another sigh, Jenna Rose said good-bye. Two little words signaled the end of life as she knew it. Just like that.

Good-bye, Savannah. Good-bye, Amy.

Good-bye to all she knew. Sure, she could keep up with her over the phone and the net. They could even send each other snail-mail stuff. But it was never going to be the same again.

Scratch one friendship, and don't expect to find another one like it.

She continued to mess with the radio, groaning at the music that came forth, as she watched the people flood from the building. "The Olsen twins meet Marilyn Manson. Check it out," she said to herself. Two girls about her age emerged from the church and started toward her car. The taller girl gave a slight smile as they passed. A black spaghetti strap dress hung over her chunky black boots and a white long-sleeve sheer blouse. Dark purple fingernails wrapped around the lacy cuffs that hung over her palms. Her hair blew slightly in the spring breeze in front of her eyes—its mouse-brown color contrasting with her sister's dyed red 'do.

The shorter one, clad in black flared pants that sparkled slight purple flecks in the sunlight and a romantic black poet's top, hurried past without a glance. Her stomach bared slightly with the sway of her arms, and her hair was spiked in various directions. Their features were the same save a slight puffiness around the cheeks for the spiky one—wide, oval eyes, high cheekbones, and thin lips. Spiky here wore considerably more makeup than her taller counterpart. Her skin had a natural, sun-brushed tan while her sister's cream color signaled a more cautious approach to the sun's rays. Both girls were clad in ample amounts of silver jewelry from their multiple-pierced ears to necklaces and rings.

The car door startled her as it swung open and her father sat down. "Did you make any friends?" he asked as he pulled his seatbelt around his middle.

"Oh yeah, tons. I'm already elected homecoming queen. I'm so popular," she replied, rolling her eyes.

"I didn't even see you trying. How about those twins? I met their father the other day. I believe you are all the same age."

She glanced over her shoulder as she reached for her seatbelt. Spiky was getting in the car behind them.

Oh yeah, what a pair we would be. Slumber party games like Light as a Feather, Stiff as a Board, painting each other's fingernails black as we listen to speed rock, and girl talk about which guy puts on his eyeliner the best. Sounds great to me. As if.

"I doubt they are my crowd, Dad."

As the Reverend Brinley started the car, he flipped the radio off. An exasperated sigh left Jenna Rose's mouth. Why couldn't he just once drive with the radio on? Normal people all over the world were driving right now, listening to music and surviving to tell the tale another day. *Why is he always so convinced that he can't do the same thing?*

"Well," he replied, matter-of-factly, as they left the parking lot, "they were in church this morning. They appear to come from a good Christian background. Sounds like they are already close enough to your crowd."

Oh yeah, that definitely makes us instant best friends.

Again with a roll of the eyes, she turned her attention to the streets outside. Neat two-story homes built around the World Wars flashed past the window—rows and rows of identical houses masquerading as unique with their differently colored shutters and various shades of tan and green siding. There was nothing short of an occasional brick version of the same house to give the neighborhood character. Different trees, bushes, and porch decorations, but basically all the same house.

Pushing the button to lower her window, she sighed loudly again. In the distance, someone was getting an early spring jump on his lawn mowing. A crisp, late March wind bit through the warm sun as she stuck her arm out the window. Maybe if she got frostbite and was about to lose a finger, her dad would have to take her back home. The hospitals here in old Hicksville couldn't be that advanced to deal with something as serious as frozen limbs. *Hey*, she thought, *they probably still use leaches.* Maybe there wasn't even a hospital here. When she was about to die and he called 911 to find out that they still worked out of the living room of the doctor's house, maybe then he'd see how stupid it was to move clear away from everything they knew. Or at least he'd learn to check on the state of medical care in the area before taking a job. Either way, he'd be sorry.

She closed her eyes and rested her head against the door of the car. How about a frostbitten ear? How would he like it if she became horribly disfigured and could never become a singer just because of a missing ear? She'd be destined to a life as a burger flipper, leading a tiny church choir filled with wannabes who couldn't carry a tune if it were handed to them. Jenna Rose found herself scoffing at her latest scenario. Sounds like the making of a movie-of-the-week—disfigured outcast everywhere but church fights all odds to make it as a singer. No one can get past her hideous looks to give her a real shot. Then, based purely on her own determination, she climbs her way to the top of the charts only to be thrown back to the gutters once it's revealed that the actress lip-syncing in her videos is not really the person singing the song. Yeah, maybe that would teach him.

The ride home was too quiet, she quickly realized. Ever since she was a little child, she loved to drive with the windows down and her head against the door. The hollow, methodic *thump, thum, thum, thump* sounds of the tires over the cobblestone street had lulled her to sleep many times.

Figures that Hicksville would have to have asphalt. Went perfect with the lack of character everywhere else.

"We're home," her dad stated cheerfully as they pulled into the driveway of 1520 Oak Drive.

Even the names of their streets are boring.

Stepping from the car, she surveyed the wooden front porch that stretched the length of their two-story World Wars–era house. Spindled white railings surrounded the uneven green-painted wood floor. The houses on either side of theirs had brick versions of the same porch.

So, there's the individuality in our home—a junky wooden porch that looks like it is about to fall in. Throw an old refrigerator, some boxes, and maybe a rotten sofa and a smelly killer dog on it, and the look will be complete—redneck shabby chic. Or better yet, trailer trash eclectic. The next hot new look for the designer remodeling shows on HGTV for sure. People will be setting their VCRs for that one.

Once again, Jenna Rose had had no input on another big decision in her life—where they would live. Amy's parents graciously hosted her at their home while he traveled up to make the necessary arrangements so she wouldn't have to miss school. He had called once or twice to get some basic input—"Would you like a one-story house? How about living right next door to your school? What do you think about having a room in the basement?" Getting in that car and heading off to, well, this, without seeing it, was the hardest thing she had ever done. She had so badly wanted to just stay with Amy and her parents. Numerous times she had tried to muster the courage to ask them to let her stay. Amy's parents loved her—she knew they would say yes. Even as she climbed in the car that last time she saw them, she wanted to run back into their arms where she could stay happy and content.

When it came down to it, she couldn't do it to her dad.

"So, what do you think?" her father asked as he opened the front door. Jenna Rose hopped slightly on one foot, testing if the wood would hold her as she ascended the stairs. "It's not going to fall in. Come on."

"Doesn't look too safe to me," she mumbled as she gingerly crossed the porch. She wondered if she could talk him into returning her to the hotel where they had stayed the past two days waiting for the house to be ready. If nothing else, at least it had safe stairs.

"The place needs a little fixing up, but nothing too serious."

Flowered paper walls and dark woodwork greeted her as she entered their new home. A strong smell of pine-scented cleaner and mothballs brought her hand to her nose. Well-worn rugs covered a battered hardwood floor through the living room and into the dining room.

"Is there an attic?" she asked as she glanced up the staircase.

"Not a livable one. But there're three bedrooms, and you can take your pick of whatever one you want."

Jenna Rose darted upstairs to survey the rooms. Her dad didn't need a really big room. It was just him. Besides, he had the whole rest of the house to keep all his stuff in. He did say she should pick the one she wanted.

After much consideration, the largest room with blue carpet and three windows was chosen. The closet was sizeable—it should fit all the important stuff. Jenna Rose grabbed her radio, popped in a CD, and went to work moving her things. "Can I paint?" she called down the staircase to her father. Clanking noises and the ruffles of newspaper told her that he was in the kitchen, putting dishes in the cupboards.

Just like him to worry about something like where the dishes go while the furniture all sat in the moving van out front.

"We'll pick you up some paint some day this week," he replied. "Some folks from the church should be over any minute to help carry the big stuff out of the van. We'll at least get your bed, dresser, and computer up there."

Sounds about right.

He was having people from the church come over before she even got her underwear out of the car.

Let's spend some quality family time together getting used to our new house—just father, daughter, and the congregation of Faith Calvary Temple. Oh yeah. And while we're at it, let's fold Jenna Rose's unmentionables while we sing campfire songs.

Exasperated, she melted into a heap on the floor and surveyed her soft yellow walls.

Who paints walls yellow with blue carpeting? Yuck.

Once she got her bed, dresser, desk, and bookshelf in the room, the walls might not scream, *"Paint me! Please put me outta my misery!"* so badly. She pulled a box to her and started to search for her posters. Maybe she could sponge it or give it a cool tie-dye effect. A little bit of yellow in layers peeking through might not look that bad. For now, the posters had to do to soften up the color. There would be time to rearrange things later. Truth was, the room was naked without her band posters up anyway. Besides, it could never officially be her room without her dream guys smiling down on her.

"Cool band," a voice said from behind her. She dropped the poster as she swung around to face the sneaky guest. A teen in black tearaways and a school wrestling shirt stood there, her computer monitor in hand. "Where you want this?"

"Anywhere," she stammered. He had the most beautiful set of eyes she had ever seen—gray with the slightest hint of blue and thick, dark lashes.

He placed the monitor under a window and stuck a hand out as he turned to face her. "Probably wondering who I am, huh?" His voice even had that deep, hunky quality that dreams were made of.

"Might have crossed my mind," she replied with a flirty smile. Fighting off the urge to reach out and touch his bouncy, sandy curls, which hung over his ears and just above his eyebrows, she grasped the hand instead and shook it.

"Parker Blevins, that's me." He stated his name so boldly and matter-of-factly, as if he expected anyone who heard him to not only know who he was but already adore him as well. Most guys who carried themselves that way just annoyed Jenna Rose.

Not this time.

Our children will be beautiful, she wanted to tell him. The words sat on the edge of her tongue waiting for their chance to spring forth. Instead, she bit her bottom lip, holding them in.

"You are Jenna Rose, right?" he asked with an amused grin. "I heard you sing at church today."

Why hadn't she found *him* to look at during the service instead of trying to decipher the mystery behind why the church had picked that shade of purple for their decor?

Would have made a much more interesting day, that's for sure.

Once again, she missed Amy. Amy would so appreciate the fact that a gorgeous guy was standing in her bedroom, and her dad had sent him there!

Mr. Overprotective down there hyperventilates when he thinks about his daughter thinking about boys.

What faith he already had in this one to send him unsupervised to his daughter's room.

Stop dreaming and talk to him before he gets bored, she reminded herself. Window of opportunity was shrinking every second.

"Your dad said you guys are from Georgia?"

She nodded. "Yep, home of the Braves and the Bulldogs." Suddenly, she was very conscious of the fact that there she stood in bare feet, a hurried ponytail, and the tank dress she had worn to church in front of this gorgeous guy in her bedroom.

What a stupid thing to say. Now he's going to think you're a sports fan or something. Like you know anything more than their names.

He smiled and bobbed his head in reply.

Look at that face. I could be a sports fan for that face.

"Hope I didn't sound too much like a screeching goose." Jenna Rose probed for some thought on how he thought she sounded. "I kind of got caught up in the whole thing and didn't realize no one else was singing at first."

"Well, you sounded great," he replied. The sound of the men below shuffling around filled the silence as they stood there in her empty room. "I better get back downstairs. We'll never get all your stuff in with me up here talking."

"Great job, doofus," she mumbled aloud to herself as he disappeared. Time to regroup and make a better impression while she still had the chance. Her father was very strict when it came to boys, and the opportunity might not arise again soon. She yanked out the ponytail and tossed the scrunchie across the room.

Running her fingers through her hair, she bounded down the staircase after him.

CHAPTER 3

Stopping briefly for the two men carrying the sofa past the staircase, Jenna Rose darted outside. Parker was in the back of the moving van collecting more of her computer parts.

Ah, I should have changed clothes before they started this moving stuff.

Problem. She didn't know where her stuff was packed away. At least, she didn't know where something flattering enough to catch his attention was at that particular moment. Sweatpants and her dad's old T-shirt—what she originally was going to put on after church—would not do the trick. Gingerly, she crawled into the back of the moving van, trying to be careful not to catch or smudge her dress on the dirty lift.

A dark oily smear about the size of a quarter appeared about where her knee hit. Scratch one cute little tank dress.

Parker held a hand out for support. His palm was soft and almost feminine, while rough spots covered his fingers.

I could hold this hand all day.

"So, tell me something exciting about Jenna Rose," he asked, leaning back against the side of the truck. "Does everyone call you 'Jenna Rose' or is it 'Jenna'?"

Trying not to be too obvious but definitely giving him the hint, she held on to his hand for just a second longer than needed and then let go. He didn't seem to notice or even care. With a shrug, she replied, "Either or, I suppose. I've always been called 'Jenna Rose,' like it was all one word

17

or something. I never really thought of it much otherwise. Maybe it's a Southern thing or something."

Or something? You sound like an idiot who can't finish a complete sentence.

"It's a beautiful name."

She found herself muttering something that could have been "thanks" or maybe even "snakes" as his eyes held hers and his brow dimpled with his smile. His mouth moved as he said something, but she was too mesmerized to catch it. Who needed posters? She could just stand him up in the corner of her room, and that would be more than enough.

"I'm a sophomore," Parker stated. "What grade are you in?"

"Sorry." She cringed in embarrassment as he sat down cross-legged on the floor of the truck. Not wanting to stain her dress any more, she pulled up a box beside him. "Freshman."

"Tell me three things about you off the top of your head without even thinking about them. Ready? Go."

This guy spends way too much time with youth ministers.

"I don't know," she found herself answering. "I had chocolate pudding for breakfast this morning at the hotel because I didn't have enough time to hit the breakfast bar. Now I have a stomachache, and I hate games like this."

Parker stretched his legs out and leaned back on his hands. "Spontaneous," he mused, nodding his head. "Cool. I see you are an old pro at these kinds of games."

Not by choice. And if we were going on your uncle's ship, I would bring jelly and butter with me. How about that?

"What about you?" Jenna Rose asked.

Tilting his head back, he stared into the sky for a moment. He stretched his legs out and held a foot up as he turned his attention back to her. "I've had these shoes for two years. I'm the youngest of three kids, and I love sour gummi worms."

Jenna Rose laughed. "You've worn the same shoes for two years?"

"Well, I haven't worn them every day for two years, if that's what you're asking," he retorted, reaching out and smacking the calf of her leg lightly.

That's the second time in the twenty minutes we've known each other that you have touched me. Prospects here seem good.

The guys who had carried their sofa in returned to the van and jabbed at Parker lightly for taking a break so soon. Awkwardly, Jenna Rose smiled at the middle-aged men as she clambered to get out of their way. Parker took her hand again as he helped her hop out of the vehicle. The men retrieved her father's filing cabinet and disappeared into the house, huffing under its heavy load.

The teen jumped back into the van with one leap and scooped up her remaining computer components. "Looks like you held me up just long enough to get me the easy job," he stated with a grin. "Pastor asked me to come along to help with the heavy stuff. They got the sofa without me, and it looks like just about everything else heavy. I guess I'm slacking." Her keyboard and tower in his arms, he hopped from the truck lift and started toward the house.

Scooping up her CD tower, Jenna Rose followed him out of the truck. "Plenty more where that came from."

"Oh no, keep holding me up." He smiled again. "You are much more interesting than your furniture, but then again, I haven't met your bookshelf yet." He thumbed in the direction of the five-shelf bookcase alone in the far right corner of the van.

Why I do declare, she wanted to reply in her best drawn-out Southern voice, *I think you might be sweet on me, Parker Blevins.*

Thanks to displaced New Englander parents, Jenna Rose had only a hint of a Georgia accent. Most people never suspected that she had spent most of her life in the South. Instead of saying something she might regret later, she let out a soft giggle to herself as she followed him up the stairs to her room.

Cute, charming, and witty. Three very endearing qualities in a guy, yes indeed.

He placed the rest of the computer by her monitor and sat down on the floor. Pleased but feigning surprise, Jenna Rose leaned against the far wall and folded her arms in front of her, trying to look uncomfortable with the prospect of a boy in her room. Perfect chance to do some more flirting and find out if this guy was as good as he looked before her dad chased him back downstairs. Honestly, she was surprised that he wasn't already up here, peeking in on his helpless little baby.

But, hey, if you can't trust the church kid willing to give up his Sunday afternoon to help some perfect strangers move into their new home, who is a pastor to trust?

Jenna Rose forced back a smile. This might work to her advantage when she went out with this guy. Nice move on his part to get in good with the pastor right from the beginning. She would have to bring it up to him someday to see what his motives really were.

Parker fumbled with his shoes, oblivious to her watching him. Once perfectly tied, he looked up and smiled. "Well, hi there."

"What? You didn't even realize that I followed you up?" She crossed her arms and put on her best pouting face.

Parker stood up and started toward the door. Turning his head slightly, he winked and grinned again. "I thought maybe it was just a cat or something." With that, he darted back down the stairs and returned to the moving.

Her feet were frozen; she was spellbound yet dumbfounded at what had just happened. Had they just exchanged some serious flirts, or was it all in her imagination? Maybe Ohio wasn't going to be so bad after all.

CHAPTER 4

With a sigh, Jenna Rose tucked her cell phone back into her purse pocket as she entered the back door. Amy wasn't home from school yet, and she really wanted to see what was going on back there. She needed to hear the voice of someone who cared about her. The big first day at Highland High was definitely a snoozer. Not only was she the new girl, but she seemed to have come down with a case of invisibility as well. It wasn't that anyone was upset she was there. Her being there was a non-issue.

She wasn't expecting a red carpet or brass band welcome or anything, but some kind of acknowledgment would have been nice. *The red-carpet welcomes are on their way soon enough,* she told herself, *when I make it big.* Then everyone would be bending over backward to welcome her.

"At least one of those *friendly* church kids or someone could have said 'hi' in the hall," she fumed. Instead, there had been nothing.

Amy, answer the phone.

She tried once more to reach her friend. Still no luck. There had to be something worth noting that she was missing back in the Peach State. Actually, just hearing Amy's voice would have smoothed over her day.

Her father's head popped out of his makeshift office—known to the previous owners of the house as the dining room. The rest of the house was full of boxes and generally disorganized and cluttered, but his office was immaculate. Even his lighthouse paintings were on the walls. Take one look in his office, and you'd swear they lived there for

21

years. Jenna Rose was sure he had even faked a layer of dust. "So, how did your first day at school go?" he asked.

"Wow, is that where I was?" Jenna Rose plopped her backpack on the kitchen table and walked to the refrigerator.

"Did you see any of the kids from church?"

Here we go again.

"Dad, I don't even know any of their names. And they don't seem to want to know mine. They don't care about me. Frankly, I don't care either. I don't know why you're so obsessed with me getting to know them." She poured two glasses of milk and grabbed the bag of chocolate sandwich cookies. As she turned the corner and came into the living room, the phone rang, and he hurried into his office to answer it. Setting their snack on the coffee table, she picked up the remote and flopped on the sofa.

Since kindergarten, Jenna Rose and her father had shared chocolate sandwich cookies after school over glasses of milk. Every day it was their *thing.* When she was younger, she would pour her heart out as they fed each other bites of their soggy cookies—each trying to master the art of soaking up just enough milk without the cookie falling to mush in the cup. She would tell him all about the kickball games at recess and how Matt Greer had kissed her while they sat on the monkey bars and how hard the day's math assignment was. When she was little, those talks were a vital part of her day. Aging somehow took away the importance of talking over the cookie tradition. Often now they just sat together, saying very little as they ate their snack. For some reason, talking wasn't necessary anymore. Just the thought of his being there was, oddly enough, comforting.

But another daily ritual she silently treasured had shrunk to maybe twice a week as her father's responsibilities to the church increased. He was always rushing out the door to be with this family at the hospital or visit with that person at the nursing home. He was everywhere but where *she* needed him to be.

As he hurried to the closet for his jacket, she downed his glass of milk in three loud gulps and slammed the glass down on the table with a deliberate thud. Picking up her own glass, she tried to focus on the television instead of looking at him.

"I have to head over to the church," he began but stopped as he saw the look on her face. He gave a weak smile and continued, "If you would start dinner, that would be great. If not, we'll see what kind of pizza they've got here in town, okay?"

She nodded without looking up from her cup.

Of course, of course, someone needed him and that's where he needed to be.

As he pulled the door closed behind him, she flipped the television to MTV, but, as usual, there was nothing on worth watching. Her father hated MTV. She couldn't particularly say that she liked it, but if it was the last thing he heard as he walked out the door, it served its purpose.

You would think a channel that called itself "Music Television" would actually play some music now and then. What a novel idea.

She flipped off the television with a sigh. The television stations here were just as bad as the radio ones.

"I guess I'll go for a bike ride," she stated out loud just to hear the sound of her own voice. The echo was rather nerve-racking. Their last house had been relatively new—a small bungalow built by their past church on the edge of one of the many historic districts. Words didn't rattle around in it like they did through the walls in this place.

Jenna Rose mounted her bike and headed the opposite way from the church.

Ohio has really weird weather, she reflected. A woman from her old church had warned Jenna Rose about the drastic swings in the weather, but she had ignored the advice, secretly happy about the idea of having real snow for holidays. Of course, she wasn't ever going to tell her dad she was excited about any possible part of this move.

It was another warmer spring day pushing the trees to bud early, but the forecast called for snow later in the week. Even with such a warm sun, the wind carried an icy sting. Walking home from the bus stop had made her hungry for more of that fresh air—even with its chill. For a

Southern girl, she enjoyed the cold on her cheeks. Amy would never be outside on a day like this if she were here. She could just picture her friend bundled up like it was twenty below, even on normal Georgia nights. She wouldn't last three minutes outside here before she would be whining about losing all feeling to her extremities.

I need to get Amy off my mind. It's not doing any good thinking about her all the time. Get over it.

Jenna Rose had not yet been able to do much exploring, and this seemed the perfect chance to take in more of the town. Besides, Parker Blevins was still on the bus when she got dropped off, so he had to live somewhere in this direction. How big could this town really be? Being the first one off the bus had a number of advantages, but Jenna Rose quickly learned that there were disadvantages as well. Like the fact that she rode the same bus as Parker. By the time she had realized Parker was sitting three rows behind her, headphones on and pencil-drumsticks pounding away on the bus seat in front of him, it was time for her to exit. She never even got the chance to catch his eye.

As Jenna Rose crossed through a traffic light, she decided to make a left away from the area she knew. *Finally! A street with some character. . .* Like her neighborhood back home with its mixture of different styles of houses, this block was a newer housing allotment, though the remnants of a *Brady Bunch* episode, with its wood and stone split-level homes, were mixed in. Small white birch trees lined the street, and houses set in different areas of the lots gave the neighborhood a more cozy appeal than the straight-in-a-line homes on her block. She found herself riding along at a leisurely pace, trying to decide which one she wished were hers and also wondering which one looked like the house Parker Blevins lived in.

She settled on a very formal-looking stone ranch house with a curved drive and perfectly manicured lawn. A silver SUV sat under a well-used basketball hoop. College banners hung on the walls of the garage, its contents neatly organized on metal shelving. She could picture the yard all decked out during spirit week and the after-game parties this house probably hosted. The whole picture screamed "star jock" home. It had to be Parker's house.

"Don't ya think it's a bit cold for a bike ride?" a familiar voice called from behind her as she turned the corner from the jock house. The voice startled her, and she came to a skidding stop.

She turned to face her crush—if that's what he was—carrying a guitar case as he bounded down the stairs of a white brick ranch house.

Guess I got that wrong.

"Do you just show up?" she asked. "You seem to be everywhere. Like some superhero or something just popping up mysteriously." She grinned ever so slightly and put a hand on her hip.

"Why? Do you need a superhero?" he asked as he continued to hop down the stairs and onto the sidewalk. He halted at the bottom of the sidewalk with his chest puffed out and his fists resting on his hips.

That's the saddest superhero pose I've ever seen, but don't you just look adorable doing it?

Jenna Rose turned her head upward and laughed deliberately. "Do I look like I need a superhero?" she asked as sarcastically as she could muster.

"Are you lost?"

"Why? Can't I ride my bike in this town? Or is that not allowed?" she countered. "Are we going to talk in questions all night?"

Her gaze was drawn to the guitar case with its Christian band stickers and inked-on graffiti. Something about the whole punk-looking guitar look didn't seem to fit the Parker she met yesterday. Then again, his baggy tan cords, red skater sneakers, and gray sweatshirt didn't really fit that guy in the wrestling T-shirt either. He had looked so preppy yesterday, and well today. . .

Maybe this isn't Parker. . .maybe he's got a brother or something. Did I meet someone else yesterday? No, it can't be. I wouldn't forget those eyes or that hair for anything.

Not that it really should matter. He was cute enough that the clothes he was wearing didn't make any real difference.

"Who said we're going to hang out all night?" came the retort. She widened her grin into a smirk. Maybe this was finally going somewhere.

She really didn't want to resort to throwing herself at him. Honestly, she had some morals.

"Well, if we're not, why are we still talking in questions? And who says we can't hang out? Did I?" she continued. "I guess it depends. . ."

"Ha," Parker broke in, pointing his finger. "I won." He broke into a sad rendition of a cabbage patch dance—his arms flopping in wild circles in front of his chest.

Oh! Please tell me he's doing that to be stupid and that's not the way he always dances.

Climbing back on her bicycle, she rolled her eyes.

His arms dropped dejectedly to his side. "Where are you going? You don't have to take off just because you lost," he continued. "You know," his pause seemed deliberate for added effect, "I think you should come with me."

This caught her attention. Planting both feet back on the ground, she asked him where he was going. Once again, she had to bite her tongue to keep from telling Parker she would follow him just about anywhere.

About time we're getting somewhere good here. Please let it be someplace cool and not like the church youth room or something. Please tell me they do something around here for fun besides read a Bible.

"Trust me. You'll like it."

"How do you know if I'll like it? You don't know me yet."

Okay. Maybe that was a little too throw-it-in-your-face obvious. But face it, cute as he was, he had been a little slow on the uptake with the flirting.

He turned away from her and started down the sidewalk. "I know you well enough to know you'll like this," he stated in a singsong manner, drawing out the word "this" into three notes.

"Follow me if you will. Just be on your merry way if you don't."

What a jerk. What a line. But, come on, look at him. How can you resist?

CHAPTER 5

As Jenna Rose watched him move swiftly down the street, she contemplated her options. She could admit defeat, follow Parker, and find out how he could possibly think he knew her already. She had to admit, she was curious what it was he was talking about. But how could this guy know her well enough to know what she would like? All he did was carry her computer up to her room and make a little small talk while tying his shoe.

That hardly constituted knowing someone.

Yeah, she *really* did want to know what it was that he thought she would like so much. And why he brought his beat-up guitar case.

But, then again, she wasn't a puppy dog who would happily wag her tail and bound along behind him and follow wherever he went. He was cute and all, but she did have some dignity. Really, how dare he walk away like that and just expect her to follow? That wasn't the kind of relationship she was looking for.

Besides, playing hard-to-get had worked really well in the past. And even though Parker seemed a little clueless at times, they would make a cute couple. And it wasn't as though she had anything else to do.

"This is stupid," she muttered as he walked farther away. Of course, going wherever he was headed was better than wandering strange streets on her bike and getting lost. She was already a little unsure of where she was. Plus, she hadn't seen one other person her age on a bike since she got here, and if she kept this up, she'd probably be the laughingstock of the whole school in just a few days.

She could hear the comments now: *Look! There goes the crazy preacher's kid with the bad Southern accent who rides her bike in circles around town all day. What a geek.*

Yeah, that would be her luck right now. Blacklisted and branded before she even got the chance to show them exactly who she was.

"All right!" she yelled. "Wait up! I'm not following behind you like a dog or something. You wait for me or I don't go." She hopped off her bike and pushed it while walking rapidly to catch up with him. He continued to walk but did slow his pace a bit.

"So, where are we going?"

"You'll see," he replied. His stride was long, and the swish of his cords broke the silence as they continued down the street. The houses varied as they walked—ranches, two-stories, and split-levels, all with well-kept lawns and individual signs of spring peeking around the corner. Small, purple, clustering flowers, looking like bunches of dark grapes, popped up through the ground in a number of yards, and new buds surrounded them. Jenna Rose never had much use for flowers. Her dad didn't have time for them, and her grandmother claimed she could kill a plastic plant put in her care. The purple flowers were really different looking. Jenna Rose found herself looking for the unusual blooms in each new lawn, comparing growth with those she had already seen.

Do something. Talk to him. Sheesh. You are looking for flowers. . . .
You are a geek.

The houses began to dwindle as they reached an aging consumer district. A strip mall with a pharmacy and empty shops sat across the street from where they were walking. Then they crossed the parking lot of a bank. An occasional car sped by, but this was far from being a busy part of town.

At last Parker turned toward a small corner pizza shop. Without a word, she followed him through the door, the smell of pepperoni arousing her stomach. The quaint little eatery was decorated in Ohio State football memorabilia. The shop was empty of customers, but several phones were ringing in the back. Three tables and a couple of booths lined one wall. A bar counter with soda coolers and a large dry-erase board filled the other wall. A middle-aged couple bustled around the kitchen while working on a large pie with the works.

"Mr. Angelino!" Parker greeted, thrusting an arm into the air. He led Jenna Rose through the restaurant to an unmarked door beside an old pinball machine in the back.

"Hey, Parker. They were starting to think you weren't coming," the thin salt-and-pepper-haired gentleman stated while spreading mushrooms quickly across his uncooked pizza.

"Ha, like that would ever happen!" Parker laughed. A deep chuckle came from the chef as well, his eyes never leaving his work.

"Parker!" called out the heavyset woman as she wiped her hands on her apron and walked toward them. "Where are your manners, son? Introduce us to your friend."

Parker stopped and set his guitar case on one of the tables. An apologetic smile appeared as he crossed the room and hugged her tightly. "Excuse me, Mrs. Angelino. This is Jenna Rose Brinley. Jenna Rose's father is the new pastor at church. Jenna, this is Mrs. and Mr. Angelino, our wonderful hosts."

Jenna Rose lit up her best smile and reached out for the woman's hand. Instead, the woman scooped her into her plump arms. "We're not much on handshaking around here, dear," Mrs. Angelino apologized cheerfully. Her warm cheek stung Jenna Rose's windburned face as the older woman pressed them together. She smelled of a mixture of pepperoni grease and lavender lotion. Surprisingly, it was a comforting combination.

"Oh! Would you like some hot chocolate, my dear? You're freezing!" the woman declared rather loudly in her ear. "Or anything to drink at all?" Without waiting for an answer, she bustled off toward the kitchen.

Parker grabbed the guitar case and held the door open. "After you," he stated.

Yeah right, like I'm walking in that door first without knowing what's on the other side. I don't think so.

"Oh no, after you," she replied.

Taking her hand in his, he led her through the door.

Now this I can handle!

Maybe this whole thing wasn't going to be a bore after all. Whatever they were doing in the back room of a pizza place, if it involved holding *his* hand, she was up for it.

F eeling like she was stuck in a B-rated action movie, Jenna Rose tightened her grip on Parker's hand. They were two crazy lovebird secret agents sneaking into the back room of some seedy joint, about to expose the bad guys.

You really need a life, Jenna Rose, you know that? At least cut back on the cheesy action flicks and do something a bit more constructive with your time.

The room was rather dark, with small beams of light dribbling through ripped holes in the browned shade-drawn windows. Old wire shelving, now forgotten and empty, lined the walls. Their footsteps echoed on the wood floor. The scent of stale air and old cardboard filled the room. Dust particles danced in the shining beams of sunlight.

Creepy.

A guy slightly taller than Parker leaned casually against the wall, tuning a bass guitar. A small beam of sunshine illuminated the cross on his black T-shirt. The whole scene reminded Jenna Rose of a cheap music video from the eighties or something. Faded letters ran above the cross on his shirt, but it was too dark for her to make out the words. His head was shaved, though there was a dark stubbly look to it. Black square-framed glasses were perched on the teenager's slight, rather thin nose. A small patch of hair ran below his bottom lip. *Almost like he forgot to shave part of his face,* she reflected. She remembered it was called a "soul patch." He was the quintessential rocker—like the guy had been completely scripted

31

right out of one of those rock-and-roll documentary shows.

Across from him sat three girls at the only table in the empty room. The teens chatted away as they studied a dog-eared notebook. Jenna Rose quickly recognized the spiky twin from the church parking lot.

Just great. . .maybe this is some strange church youth room or something.

Jenna Rose studied the door. Noticing her hesitation, Parker gave her hand a slight squeeze, and electricity jumped through her body. She again wrapped her fingers around his, having no intention of letting go even as the disappointment rushed through her veins.

He thinks my idea of fun is a Bible study or something. Typical though. No one actually thinks a P.K. can have any real fun.

Parker released her hand and plopped his guitar case in the middle of the girls' table. "About time you showed up," one girl mumbled light-heartedly. She pushed his case in fake disgust and stood up. Her dark brown hair was done up in dozens of thin braids that were pulled out of her face with a red bandana. A gray T-shirt tightly covered her thin body. Her army-green pants were oversized with bulky pockets on the knees. Flimsy plastic bracelets covered her wrists.

On second thought, maybe it's a séance or something freaky like that.

Jenna Rose fidgeted with her coat, unsure of what was expected of her. Why didn't she just stay home and watch MTV like she started to? That way she could just laugh at the freaks without risk of bodily harm.

Lifting her hands in a mock fighting stance, the girl continued, trying to sound tough in spite of the big smile on her face: "Don't make me have to lay the smack down on you next time, boy. You show up when you're supposed to."

Parker reached out with the hand that had been holding Jenna Rose's and grabbed the girl around the back of the neck. She squealed and tried to wiggle away from his grasp. Drawing her close to him in a tight bear hug, he turned back to Jenna Rose. "Jenna, this is Shanice."

Okay. So he's one of those grabby types that's all over every girl he's around?

The girl struggled to release herself from his grip. With a quick wave in their guest's direction, she wrapped her arm around his waist and attempted to turn herself around. Parker simply used the opportunity to strengthen his hold on her. "Shanice thinks she's a wrestling sup-a-star." Lifting from his knees nearly effortlessly, he brought her up to his shoulder and barked with a grin in her ear. "But she's just sorry." As he dropped her back to her feet, he pulled the bandana off her head and whirled it around on his hand. His opponent stretched her neck to one side and then the other before she grabbed his arm. Shanice's braids flopped in front of her eyes.

That must have taken forever to do. Jenna Rose admired her. *I wouldn't have the patience to sit still that long.*

There were at least a hundred braids in her hair. Parker nestled the fabric back on her head, making sure the braids still covered her eyes. "Sorry or not, I still love her. She's been one of my best friends for like five minutes." His laughter lit his whole face up.

Shanice smacked her lips and rolled her eyes dramatically. "Please," was her only response.

Parker turned his attention to the other girls. He nudged the spiky one from the church parking lot in the shoulder. Biting at her lip, she bumped her head back into his stomach and returned her attention to the paper in her hand. "That's Andi."

Jenna Rose found something about her to be a bit intimidating, but she smiled as best she could and said hello.

Anyone who purposely colors their hair the same color as Clifford and styles it to stand straight up and straight back off their head can't be all there. And the whole Christian vampire clothing thing was just plain weird.

Keeping an eye on the wrestling match, Andria raised her head toward the newcomer, her eyes sizing the "new girl" up. Jenna Rose detected a hint of disapproval in the other girl's body language. It seemed to say, *How dare you bring someone in our exclusive little freak clubhouse.* Again, Jenna Rose tugged at her coat. Maybe if she tried hard enough, it would swallow her up and beam her back home—like all the way to Savannah.

Stop looking at me, you freaky weirdo.

Andria seemed to delight in her discomfort momentarily, and then her face softened. "Hi," she stated, diplomatically. "You're the one from church, right? Your dad's the new pastor?"

Mustering up another smile, Jenna Rose nodded.

The one from church. Great. That's what I'm going to be known as?

Next Parker pointed to the girl standing farthest from them. "And that's her sister Darby."

Jenna Rose hadn't yet noticed the taller twin was there beside her sister, fiddling with a notebook and pencil. Darby waved, her fingernails still the deep purple they were Sunday.

"Over there is Elijah, and Amber is probably around here some-where," Parker continued. A hand popped up from behind some speak-ers and a mixing board. Drums sat beside them. "There she is."

Oh, I am definitely not in the right universe.

Jenna Rose tried to smile without showing her discomfort. Punk rock wannabes and skater guys were just not her crowd—they always frightened her. Weren't they the kind of people who ended up shoot-ing up schools and stuff like that? Amy would just die if she could see her now.

Then again, if Amy were here, I wouldn't be within a hundred feet of this place.

"You can sing, I hear," Shanice stated calmly as she looked her up and down too. Not one to generally feel self-conscious, Jenna Rose squirmed a bit under the girl's careful gaze.

No use prolonging it. Kick me out. Cast your spells, chant your voodoo, or light your candles—whatever it is you're gonna do.

No one else seemed to notice her uneasiness.

Getting to her feet, Andria stuck her hand out to their guest. "Call me Andria or Andi. . .it doesn't matter to me."

Jenna Rose shook her hand and smiled.

Just don't hurt me, whatever it is you do.

Andria pulled her hooded sweatshirt over her head to reveal a Strawberry Shortcake baby tee. Stuffing the rest of the candy bar in her mouth, she grabbed up her drumsticks, saying quickly, "Let's get busy, guys."

"We're glad you dropped by. We need to go play," Darby said kindly and then made her way to an acoustic guitar leaned up against a barstool. With the instrument in hand, she perched herself on the stool.

Jenna Rose replaced the twins at the table as the group assembled themselves around the drum set. She pulled her legs up to her chest and wrapped her arms around them. With a sigh, she leaned her chin on her knee in her favorite thinking position.

So Parker Blevins knows me well enough to think I would like to watch his garage band practice? He has a little bit more to find out.

Did she honestly look like a high school garage band groupie? No.

Please. I have bigger things going than cheering on some wannabes.

Andria tapped her sticks together and then started in with a rhythm. Following with the bass, Elijah turned toward the drummer and nodded his head with the beat. Darby and Parker brought in the melody on guitar. Jenna Rose closed her eyes, focusing on the music for a moment. They weren't bad at all. Actually, they were pretty good.

Just as Shanice was about to sing, Parker stopped playing. "Hold on a sec, guys. I've got an idea. Jenna, you know this song?" he called.

No one back home ever called her Jenna. At first she didn't even realize he was talking to her. If he kept this up, it was really going to take some getting used to.

But of course I know this song. I'm a preacher's kid, and I've wasted too many summer days in church camps. Just try to find a song sung by Chris Tomlin I don't know. Duh.

She nodded in return.

Parker looked around at the others. "You guys don't mind? I want to hear them sing it together. It's really a song with a two-part harmony."

Elijah nodded in agreement and moved his microphone to the center of the area. Jenna Rose crawled out of her fetal position and stepped forward, looking at the other vocalist awkwardly. Shanice didn't look too pleased.

Sorry, chick, it's time for a real voice to do it.

"Jenna, you take the lead then," Parker instructed. "Shanice, you just go with it. Let's see what we have."

Again, they started the music. Jenna Rose could feel the eyes of her counterpart on her as she began the song.

She's gonna lay the smack down on me is what she's gonna do.

"Over the mountains and the seas," she sang as she let her eyes fall shut. Just her song and her. With that, she was engrossed.

Shanice has beautiful skin, Jenna Rose reflected after they had finished the first verse. The other girl fumbled with the microphone. Jenna Rose was always slightly jealous of girls who didn't need tanning beds or long periods in the sun to have a deep, glowing complexion. Spending whole days under rays would never accomplish that tone on her. But, then again, that girl's color had to be natural—Native American or Middle Eastern or something. You couldn't fake that shade with a bottle or a tanning bed. That was the kind of color that took an exact science to conjure up and an entire summer to perfect. And most people—present company included—often failed miserably at it.

As Shanice joined in for the chorus, the door opened and Mrs. Angelino emerged, carrying a pizza and a pitcher of soda. She looked as if she were going to burst with excitement as she stood over the table momentarily, watching them play and sing together. With a slight clap and a giggle, she hurried back through the door.

A moment later she reappeared with glasses of ice and placed them on the table. Cupping her hands together in front of her, she smiled as she watched them perform. "Bravo! Bravo!" she cried as they came to a close. "Guys, I think you have found it. You have really found it! That," she took Darby's hand in hers and squeezed, "was God-breathed, if I ever witnessed it. Now take a break and get some pizza while it's still hot. You can't do it on an empty stomach."

The group closed in on the pizza, thanking their host for her kind words. Hugs and high fives were exchanged around her as Jenna Rose stood awkwardly in the middle of the room, not sure if she should leave the microphone or not.

"You haven't had pizza until you've had Angelino's," Parker stated as he pushed her along to the table. "Come on."

The group stood around the table, chatting excitedly. All their warmth and friendship toward one another reminded her even more that her friends were hundreds of miles away. Even among their laughter, Jenna Rose felt completely alone.

Why aren't they eating?

Everyone seemed to just be looking at the pizza. She hated not being in the loop.

Elijah's lowered head quickly gave her the answer. Parker slipped his hand in hers and a spark made its way up her spine. His hand was so warm and soft, yet manly all at the same time. His touch was just amazing every time she felt it. She gave it a quick squeeze, hoping he would pick up on her signal. The spark quickly faded as Darby reached for her other hand. They were making a big circle, nothing more.

"Heavenly Father," Parker stated, his voice barely above a whisper, "we thank You for the chance to come before You as one in Christ. We praise You for the gifts You have given us and ask that You would continue to guide us to use them to glorify Your name. We thank You for new friends and old, praising You for the chance to fellowship with other Christians. Please bless this food to the nourishment of our bodies and bless the hands that prepared it. In Jesus Holy Name, Amen."

"Amen," the others stated together. As soon as they lifted their heads, many hands started grabbing for the steaming pizza.

Jenna Rose mustered an uneven smile as Darby handed her a piece of the cheese pizza.

What have I gotten myself into? I am so out of here.

Night was settling in as the group parted ways. Parker and Elijah walked with Jenna Rose as she pushed her bike and worried about going home. *I am so dead. I didn't even leave him a note where I was going to be. He'll flip out! I can see it now—the church search party will be out and about, scouring the entire city.*

When she got home, she was going to get it.

Then again, what could he really do? Ground me? Please. From what?

She was hundreds of miles away from the home that mattered and everyone important to her. Amy hadn't picked up the phone in twenty-four hours. The only people who had shown any interest in her were Bible-beating sideshow freaks. And the best-looking guy she had ever seen appeared dead to her come-ons. She was going through enough on her own, thank you very much.

She mounted her bike quietly, contemplating whether to just start peddling and get home out of the cold and forget this whole thing with Parker or stick out the ride and see what was going on. She knew what the answer was going to be. She peddled slowly, trying to match their pace.

Elijah was taller but less muscularly defined than his friend. "Man, it's cold," he complained, yanking the collar of his blue work-style jacket up around his ears. A patch with the name "Joe" embroidered on it sat on his chest. She wondered if Elijah even knew Joe or if this was one of those *cool* things she didn't quite get.

"You wouldn't be so cold if you wore a hat," Parker retorted, giving his black ski cap a tug. He just looked so cute with his curls tumbling out the sides. That hair was just adorable. . .though she still hadn't touched those curls yet. Oh, but she would.

"Or had some hair." For this added comment, Elijah punched him in the arm. Parker just grinned again and turned his attention to her. "Elijah had some great hair, let me tell you."

"Yeah? What happened?" She could pretend she cared if it was going to impress Parker. She'd feigned interest in NASCAR, football, tennis, even chess to catch the interest of a guy—she could spend a few minutes acting like she really cared about what happened to the hair of Parker's friend.

The would-be rocker looked thoroughly embarrassed as he studied the tips of his Airwalks. "Ever heard of dyeing with Kool-Aid?" Parker didn't wait for her to answer. "Well, mixing pink lemonade with tropical punch to get the right shade is a bad idea. Oh man, was it a hideous color!"

Leaning on his friend, Parker looked at Jenna Rose and winked. He obviously was enjoying retelling his friend's misfortune. "But, oh, did he smell good."

Even Jenna Rose found herself laughing this time. "Sorry," she spit out as she tried to regain her composure.

"Anyways," Elijah shot her the dirtiest look he could through his own laughter, "it like fried my head. My hair was so brittle. It'd break off out of nowhere. I finally decided to shave it off and start new."

Jenna Rose thought his current style rather suited him—Elijah looked a bit odd and mysterious. For some reason she just couldn't picture the quiet bass guitarist with flaming pink hair. She found it humorous the way he tugged at his oversized blue work pants every few steps. Somebody needed to teach this crew how to find the right-sized clothes.

The boys talked as they walked along, chatting about video games, music, and a funny incident that happened to them during lunch. It seemed obvious that the pair was good friends as they joked around, poking and prodding one another at times. Jenna Rose wondered how long they had known one another. The whole group seemed really tight.

"What's the name of the band?" she finally asked, wishing Parker would focus his attention back on her. If it took talking about his little garage band to get him to pay attention to her, she'd do it. *Sounds like I'm a groupie already.* They were moving very slowly, but all the same, they were still heading toward home. Her time with him was slowly ticking away.

Parker shrugged. "We haven't come up with one yet. What do you think would be a good name for a Christian band?"

"Besides Newsboys, Jars of Clay, and dc talk," Elijah added. "Seems those are already taken."

Jenna Rose gave him a weak smile. *Huh huh, that was hilarious.* "I don't know. What are your choices?" She brought her bike to a standstill. They were treading so slowly, she couldn't keep it upright anymore.

"We don't really have any yet that we all agree on," Parker replied.

"And no one seems to like 'The Elijah Show,'" his friend mumbled. "I think it has a ring to it."

Parker grabbed him by the back of the head and pretended to throw him headfirst into a tree. Obviously it was a stunt they had practiced before. Elijah snapped his head back and stumbled backward, holding his head tightly. "See the abuse I have to take?"

She shook her head in response. "I'm not much of a Christian music fan," Jenna Rose apologized. "I find most of it is just a rip-off of real music."

Elijah popped up out of his act. "Real music?" he demanded. "So. . . what? We're just second-rate musicians then?" He smacked Parker on the chest. "That's it. Since we don't play 'real music.'"

"I didn't mean that," she pleaded. She looked at Parker quickly. Was he also offended?

He's not saying anything. Just great. He is.

"We'll call ourselves 'Second Rate,'" Elijah said dejectedly.

Parker started to laugh. "Dude, that's not right. We'll keep looking."

The electric guitar player continued to mumble under his breath as

Jenna Rose studied Parker's face for some kind of sign as to what he was thinking. She honestly didn't mean to offend anyone. Didn't everyone realize Christian music was nothing more than a bad copy of regular music? That's why the Christian bookstores had those "If-you-like-Eminem-you'll-like-KJ52" posters everywhere. That's how they reeled people in—by trying to sound like well-known musicians.

The guys continued to poke and prod one another with Elijah throwing in a "second rate" comment every now and then. Parker just shoved him back and said little.

"You guys are too much for me," she finally stated as she climbed on her bicycle. She rode slowly, staying within earshot of the two. Not being sure exactly how far she had to go before making a turn, she didn't want to get lost. She didn't need that on top of not telling her dad where she was. He was probably going to freak already over the fact that she was with not just one but two boys. He might trust one church boy, but the fact that there were two would give him a coronary. He seemed to think that by having two or more boys together, they not only forgot how to use their brains but also lost control over all moral abilities. But these guys were her safe ticket home, and she couldn't afford to lose them and not find her way back.

Besides, there was another more important reason to hang around. Like finding out if Parker had anything to say about her.

"Today went well," Parker stated after a short silent period. Jenna Rose slowed down, trying to catch as much of what was being said as possible.

Elijah shifted his backpack on his shoulder and nodded. "I have to agree. She's good."

"I told you she was."

"You haven't, like, asked her to join officially yet or anything, have you?"

"Not yet. I wanted all of your input first. Wow, what a voice. But I wanted to know what you thought."

He thinks I have an awesome voice. He thinks I have an awesome voice!

41

Jenna Rose was beaming. Ha, she could take all the punishment in the world from her dad. Parker Blevins thought enough about her awesome voice to make sure his friends found out about it.

Elijah scratched his head and sighed. "All I can say is: How is Shanice going to take this?"

Who cares? Who cares?

Parker stuffed his hands into his pockets and hurried in front of his friend. Walking backwards, he continued to plead his case. "Elijah, do you really understand what we have here? Jenna is the one thing we were missing. We're good on our own, but this girl takes us over the top. I mean, we're going to go from a coffeehouse praise band to the big time. There's no doubt about it at all now. I can feel it! As much as we might hate to admit it, it has little to do with us and everything to do with that girl's voice up there. Shanice will be okay. She's got a good voice, and I think they sounded great together. There's no reason Shanice has to go anywhere."

"And I hope she doesn't. Yeah, I liked her voice too," his friend interrupted. "But it's just not right. Shanice has been here since the beginning. I hate to see her get a bum rap. It's shady, man."

A skateboard was parked on the sidewalk in front of them, while other abandoned toys were strung across the front lawn of a small white cottage. Parker stepped up on the board, balanced for a second, and then popped up the tail end in perfect ollie form.

Jenna Rose closed her eyes and shook her head slowly. This was unbelievable.

He really is a skater boy. Amy would just die. I'm falling for a skater rock star wannabe. What in the world am I doing?

"I saw that! Don't look so surprised," he stated as he tossed a pinecone in her direction, another big grin on his face. He pushed the skateboard back toward the house and continued walking. "I'm a man of many talents."

"Is that what you call it?" she asked, flashing a smile.

"Well, something like that." Again, he dug his hands deep into his pockets and shrugged his shoulders.

Elijah held a hand over his mouth as he laughed. "Don't let him fool ya. Give me ten minutes of your undivided attention, and I could teach even you how to do an ollie."

The bike came to an abrupt stop as she planted her feet and made a silent chuckle motion.

Why am I still with these guys again? Even me? Like, how hard could that really be? And what would possess you to think that I would even be interested in learning?

"No disrespect," he gasped between breaths. "I really should get back. I'm on the clock now." After bumping fists with Parker, Elijah gave a wave in Jenna Rose's direction and sprinted back toward the pizza shop.

Parker watched him go and then turned his attention back to Jenna Rose. Noticing the look of confusion on her face, he explained, "Mr. and Mrs. Angelino are Elijah's uncle and aunt. He stays with them. He has parents with some real issues."

Don't we all?

Jenna Rose dismounted her bike again and walked alongside him. "That's great, you know, that they let you guys use that room like that for practice. They seem like really good people."

"Yeah, Mrs. Angelino was tired of us taking up her whole basement, I'd say. I think it was more for her benefit than our own that they gave it to us. I'm not complaining though. Most bands struggle for a place to stay, and we don't even have to tear our stuff down or anything. Elijah would like to turn that room into a little Christian coffeehouse where we'd play on weekends, but I think the Lord has bigger plans for us. It's a cool idea and all, but I don't think it's our calling to play there."

"Yeah?" she asked as she caught sight of his house. "What makes you think God has anything to do with this?"

No! We can't be here already! That is so not fair.

Maybe if she kept him talking, he would walk her all the way home. She didn't want to end this day any sooner than she had to.

"Yeah." He turned and looked at her. Eye to eye for the first time, her heart pulsed harder and harder. Once again, Jenna Rose found herself mesmerized by his eyes. She wanted to kiss him. Her body tingled with anticipation.

No, no, check that.

She wanted him to kiss her even more. The electricity she felt when he touched her hand wasn't enough. Those were just like little teases. She wanted to feel that way all the time. There were times that he just didn't seem to be picking up on her signals in the past few days, but he had to get it now. Her heart skipped a beat as he raised a hand to her face and gently brushed her windblown hair from her eyes. Even that slight touch of his hand was heaven-sent. Looking at her very confidently, Parker stated, "He sent us you, didn't He?"

CHAPTER 8

Every inch of Jenna Rose wanted to scream as they headed up her driveway.

What am I going to have to do to get him to see that I like him? I just don't understand this guy at all. What in the world was all that about back there if it wasn't going to lead to hooking up? And what was wrong with this guy that he wasn't taking advantage of the situation regardless of his feelings? There was little doubt it was all supposed to lead to a kiss. Guys didn't just stand there and look at a girl that way without wanting something.

So what went wrong?

Looking at her square in the face was the closest that he came to making a move. But at least that was a step up—he hadn't stopped long enough to look at her for real before that. The moment had been perfect. She just didn't get why he didn't go for it. Any other guy she had ever known would have been all over the chance!

He wanted her to join the band. That much was obvious. He had danced around the real question, seeming to get a feel for what she would answer when he did ask. His vision was big. They were going big-time, he was sure. Darby, the one with the notebook and pen, was their writer and guitarist, and she had books full of lyrics, he said. Her stuff was good, he kept pointing out. Real God-inspired lyrics. All of the band members were skilled on their instruments and put worshipping God through their musical abilities first. Parker knew. It was just a matter of time before they were discovered. And Jenna Rose was the key to it all. He might not have said it to her, but she had heard him say it to Elijah.

Deep down, she wished she had that much confidence in something. Even in her own singing, she knew she had the talent. But anyone who watched *Behind the Music* or *Driven* enough times knew it took more than talent. It took the right career choices, a bit of selfishness, and a lot of luck. Being part of a Christian garage band didn't seem like a good career choice to her.

Jenna is the one thing we're missing. I mean, we are going to go from a coffeehouse praise band to the big time.

Those words of his to Elijah kept rolling around in her head. He never asked her to join, and she didn't bring it up. Singing with them was fun, but she had plans of her own. Her future didn't involve Christian music. Christian music was fine and good for church camps and revivals, but she was looking for more of a career than that. Her plans were for real music.

Her father's car wasn't in the driveway. Relief washed over her temporarily. He probably hadn't even left church yet.

"Thanks for walking me home," she said, unsure of what she should do next.

"Your dad home?" Parker asked.

"No, he's probably still at work."

Or then again, he's out there hunting for me. I am so dead. Shoulda kissed me when you had the chance, Parker. I'm not gonna see the outside of my room until I'm twenty-five.

Parking her bike in the garage, she offered him the chance to come inside and warm up a bit. *If I'm going to go down, I might as well go down big.* As the sun had departed, every bit of warmth in the air went with it. Parker's cheeks were rosy, and his hands were buried deep in his pants pockets. He looked miserable. Jenna Rose reached out and touched his red face. It was cold and as soft as his hands. "You're freezing," she whispered. "Come in and have a hot chocolate."

"I should just get home," he replied. "The sooner the better."

He's slipping away again. . . .

"You sure? My dad should be home later, and he could drive you back. You can use the phone to call your parents. I make a mean hot chocolate." Jenna Rose couldn't honestly remember the last time she made hot chocolate. Hot chocolate was hardly the beverage of demand in Georgia. She was reaching for any straws she could find now to keep his attention. But really, how hard could it be to open a bag and dump it into hot water?

He smiled a weak smile and nodded. "Thanks for the offer, but I'll have to take a rain check. I really need to get home."

"You sure? I really could use the company." The last line came out almost in a whisper. There was no going back now if he said yes.

Kiss him. Kiss him now. Show him that you mean business.

"I'll save you a seat on the bus tomorrow," he stated as he walked back down the driveway. Jenna Rose waved as he headed away. As he reached the end, he turned around. "I would really like to hear you sing some more. You're welcome at the shop anytime. But now I really should go."

Jenna Rose raised a hand again as he turned his attention down the street. A scream welled up inside of her, begging to be let out. Taking a deep breath, she stifled it. He had turned down an invitation into her empty house. She wanted to bang her head on the doorframe. She *needed* to scream. This was all just insane.

But he had sounded like he hoped to see her again.

Maybe I smell funny or something.

She laughed at herself as she closed the door behind her.

Through the window, she watched as Parker headed down the street. Off in the distance, he bent over to play with the skateboard again. He mounted the board and took off into the street doing more jumps and moves that she didn't quite understand.

Time to move on. He's not interested plus he's not my type.

How did that song go? *He was a skater boy. . . .*

There was truth in music—that fact she had seen a long time ago. Maybe it was too early to give up on him already. She'd wait him out a bit longer and see what happened. It wasn't like she had much else to do.

The hearty smell of stew greeted her as she opened the kitchen door. Sometime since she left for her bike ride, her dad had been home and put dinner in the Crock-Pot, but there was no sign it had been recent. Inside, things looked as she had left them. The plate and glass from her cookie snack were still in the sink. He would have washed those had he been home for any length of time—he had this thing about dirty dishes. There was no sign he had found her gone and was now on a massive manhunt through the neighborhood. For once she was glad he was at work instead of being here waiting for her. She didn't need to deal with him right now as well.

Grabbing an apple on her way past the fruit bowl, she bounded up the stairs two at a time. Her head ached with a bit of embarrassment and some confusion, but mostly what almost felt like anger. Guys just didn't do this to Jenna Rose Brinley. After this emotional roller-coaster ride, the only thing she wanted to do was take a long bath, head to bed, and get as much rest as she could before school in the morning. She needed to get her mind off this whole mess.

Except she couldn't.

In the bathtub, she found herself going over and over the whole afternoon's scenario in her head. What went wrong? He wanted to kiss her. There was a hunger there in his arms too. They had twitched ever so slightly when he had reached up and touched her face. He wanted to wrap his arms around her—she could almost hear his arms screaming for it. His body was aching to hold her, which was why he could do little more than whisper when he spoke.

But why wouldn't he go through with it? What's a kiss anyway? I've kissed more than one guy with a lot less chemistry than that and not thought twice about it.

Or. . .what if he told somebody?

What could possibly be more embarrassing than being turned down? Only having the whole school know about it!

That's going to be my luck. Everyone's going to know I got shot down, and then what are they going to think of me?

As she wrapped her dad's thick plaid bathrobe around herself, a thought that made her heart sink came to her. He didn't want to kiss her because she was a P.K. That had to be it! It had to be because of her dad being the pastor.

Good churchgoing girls don't go around kissing guys on street corners in Ohio, I suppose. Ugh, this whole Christian thing.

CHAPTER 99

A knock startled her from a deep sleep. Groggily, Jenna Rose glanced out from under her blanket to find bright sunlight spilling through her windows. That hadn't happened in forever—a full night's sleep. Well, not since she was forced out of her nice warm first-floor bedroom in sunny Georgia and moved into this old drafty second-story room in freezing Ohio.

Yanking the pillow up over her head, she burrowed back down into her comforter. It was a Saturday morning. Wasn't anything sacred with this man? If there's no place to be on a Saturday morning, then there's no reason to get out of bed. Plain and simple. It's the teenage way.

"I'm not here," she called at the sound of the third knock. "Leave a message and I will get back to you when I decide to get up. Night-night." He hated it when she got sarcastic.

The door opened slowly. Startled and a bit annoyed, Jenna Rose lifted the corner of her pillow and peered from underneath. Her dad never just walked into her room. That was one thing she could give him—he respected her privacy when it came to her bedroom. Something had to be pretty serious for him to just barge in like that.

Oh great. Darby McKennitt's head appeared through the door. Today her hair was done up in twisties with brightly colored rubber bands on the ends. She was wearing a pretty normal looking pair of jeans and a gray sweatshirt. They caught each other's glance for a moment before Jenna Rose settled the pillow back down on her face.

Maybe she'll think I'm still asleep and just go. It's too early in the morning to deal with this girl.

"Hi," Darby stated quietly, a hint of uncertainty in her voice. "Your dad told me to come on up. I hope that's okay. I guess he thought you were already up and getting ready." The door closed at the end of her sentence. From within her warm hideaway, Jenna Rose could hear her unwanted guest move across the room, creaking the telltale floorboard near her dresser.

Okay, first you enter my room uninvited, and now you're checking it out?

Jenna Rose snorted lightly as she pretended to snuggle into a sleepy ball. It always worked with her dad. Assuming that she had been talking in her sleep, he would tiptoe out and pull the door closed behind him. It was always worth at least a couple more hours of peace.

"Well," the girl continued.

Can't you see I'm trying to sleep here? Who invited you into my room anyway?

"I know you haven't come to youth group or anything yet," Darby continued. "Your dad said last week you've just been taking some time to settle in, but that you'd start coming soon."

My dad said. . . What are you doing talking to my dad? That just figures. He hardly has enough time to share a meal with his only child, but I'm sure he's spent plenty of time with you solving your little weirdo-chick problems. That's my dad—always out to save the world—but he's losing his own kid in the shuffle.

"I thought maybe today would be a good day to start."

The sound of Darby's voice was starting to hurt Jenna Rose's head. She wanted to sit up, throw off the pillow, and say point blank, "Look, I hate youth groups. I don't want to be in your stupid youth group. I don't want to do your dumb games. I don't want to serve spaghetti or baby-sit kids. I'm not going to starve all night for some probably imaginary third-world kid. Just go away and let me sleep. Maybe I'll wake up in Savannah, and you'll just be a figment of my imagination, okay?"

But, of course, all she did was fake another snore.

Gotta be the perfect girl, you know.

Preacher's kids always have to be the perfect kids, the role models all the other church kids strive to be. Which meant she could only stall joining this youth group for a little while longer. It was just a matter of time before she ran out of excuses and found herself there. "People will wonder what's wrong with the youth group if the pastor's own child isn't involved in it," her father had already said a couple times. "It's a good, strong youth group, and you'll benefit from it as much as they'll benefit from you being a part of it."

Like she cared.

"We're doing a mission project," Darby continued. "Should be fun." The sad thing was her tone said she completely believed this was the best possible way for them to spend a Saturday together—shoveling dirt at some Habitat house or being immersed in suds up to your pits while scrubbing dishes in a soup kitchen.

I've done it enough times and haven't found it fun yet. If you would have barged in here and woke me up saying, "Let's go see a movie," I may have had a different outlook on you. But instead, I just want you out.

This time the snort from under the blankets was louder, a slight snore drifting off her lips for good measure. Like she was getting out of bed on a Saturday to go work with a bunch of people she didn't know. Besides, she had dance team tryouts this afternoon.

"Well, I should be going, I guess." Jenna Rose heard the sigh of her door on its hinges. "We'll be at the church until after lunch. I hope to see you there. You know all the guys from the band, and everyone else is really excited about meeting you. We have a good time together. They're a riot."

Yeah. . .I bet they are. Buh–bye.

CHAPTER 10

Nearly an hour later, she awoke with a start. Parker Blevins was in that youth group, and she had just turned down the chance to spend part of the day alongside him! Why didn't she think of that before? Burying her hands behind her head, the urge to smother herself with her pillow washed over her as she stared at the ceiling.

Could you really smother yourself with your own pillow? Or would you just knock yourself out and relax your grip unconsciously and start breathing again?

The little swirling patterns on the ceiling were a bit hypnotizing when you really studied them. . .or wanted to block out how stupid you felt. She found herself entertained by the patterned ceiling a lot lately.

She needed to talk to Amy. Two weeks had passed since she had last heard her voice—almost a month since she had seen her best friend's face. Maybe she would talk to her dad about going to Amy's for awhile in the summer. Or maybe Amy could come to Ohio. Either option was fine with Jenna Rose. She needed her best friend now more than ever.

Jenna Rose was lovesick. All over some guy with an addictive smile and hair like that dude who almost won the first *American Idol*. She could see Amy now. "He's just trying to rip off that show," she would state, trying to ease her friend's pain with some witty humor. "Rock star wannabe, get your own look." Amy wasn't a P.K. She was therefore afforded the luxury of being able to speak her mind without risking constant disapproval, usually from some church busybody who had no business worrying about what was said. Amy often said the things Jenna Rose was too afraid even to say in her head.

The thought of dance team tryouts dragged her from bed. She would whine about Parker later. Right now, it was time to get ready for the show—time to get around her crowd and show the people at this school exactly what Jenna Rose Brinley was all about. Her time was well overdue.

She pulled on a pair of gray cotton pants. The last guy she dated had loved these pants with their slim cut and just enough bagginess to leave her shape to the imagination. Jenna Rose loved the way they rested just below her belly button and fastened with thin white tie cords. Back in Savannah, she often wore them with a sports bra and the short jacket that went with the pants. Of course, she liked to find excuses to tie the jacket around her waist as often as possible, especially if any guys were in the vicinity. Since this was a school function, she would tone it down with a sporty-looking baby tee instead.

A spicy combination of cinnamon French toast and sage sausage beckoned her to head downstairs and join her dad for brunch instead of fussing over her hair, but today's tryouts were too important not to make sure she looked just right. Besides, if she had heard him right, he had a Bible study group or something else church-related meeting down there. *That's reason enough to stay in bed Saturday morning.* Scooping all of the essentials off the top of her dresser and into her shower bucket, she cranked up the radio and headed into the bathroom.

"Can you turn that down some, please?" her dad called from the living room. Jenna Rose pretended not to hear him. If it were some old Beatles' song or a hymn, he wouldn't care, but no music even slightly influenced by hip-hop should be played in his house. Besides, she could barely even hear it in the bathroom. And she needed it right now to get psyched for the dance team tryouts.

Making the team wasn't going to be a problem. She had that done already. Jenna Rose Brinley danced nearly as well as she sang. No, she wasn't concerned at all about the tryouts themselves; she was worried about having a real reason to be around the kind of people she should be hanging out with. This was her chance to get things right with her world.

Back home, I wouldn't be worrying over this kind of stuff.

As she brushed her hair in long, deliberate strokes, her mind drifted to Savannah and what she would be doing right now if she were still there. She would have been showered and ready at sunup. Amy was a morning person, which made Jenna Rose an early riser by association. They would have been gone hours ago doing something. The two friends would probably have been scoping out boys at the mall or practicing their dance team moves. It wouldn't really have mattered what it was because, with Amy, it would have been a good time.

Satisfied with her hair in a ponytail that was secured back through the scrunchie so it didn't hang loose on her neck, she started on her makeup. At a younger age, she had loved to watch *anybody* put makeup on. Amy's mom had done her face up for the first time at Amy's eleventh birthday slumber party. Jenna Rose was mesmerized from that moment on. Magazines gave her most of her application tips—men as dull as her dad didn't have any tricks to share. In addition, the sight of Jenna Rose wearing makeup was too much of a reminder to him that she was growing up, so it was just easier to pretend its existence wasn't important. Jenna Rose knew better. Her mom was gone long before Jenna Rose was old enough to appreciate the intricacies of wearing eye shadow, but she still remembered how her mom had brightened up any room she entered.

"Your beauty is true from God," her father used to always say when his only child would ask repeatedly for makeup at the store. "You don't need that stuff. It should be that of your inner self, the unfading beauty of a gentle and quiet spirit, which is of great worth in God's sight."

Yeah, God's sight. That gets you lots of dates.

She'd worry about God's idea of beauty when the time came. Right now was a different story. And Jenna Rose really found it annoying when he spouted Scripture like it was his own words or something.

In truth, her father was right for the most part about the makeup. Like she remembered of her mother, Jenna Rose usually got away with little more than a cover-up to level her skin tone out, some glitter for shimmer around her eyes, and a good lip gloss. The only thing better than having beauty was achieving it in minimal time and effort. Still, looking better than most of the other girls in your school was always a nice added bonus.

She tossed her lip gloss in her backpack and bounded down the stairs. The radio still blared from her room, but she pretended not to notice. If he had to yell at her to turn it off, at least he'd stick his nose out of his office long enough to do that. He couldn't take his focus away from the churchies for too long—they might have to think for themselves or something for a moment.

Her kitchen was full of people. A group of middle-aged women sat around the table picking at a bowl of fruit and taking notes in their booklets. Folding chairs were set up haphazardly, all in her way, and three men wearing college sweatshirts stood around the island sipping coffee from foam cups. The lingering smell of French toast tugged at her empty stomach, but she saw no evidence of its existence other than the dirty plates stacked here and there. One lone piece of sausage sat dejectedly in a bowl on the countertop.

Figures that he wouldn't even save her any.

In the living room, two preschool-aged children jumped on her sofa with dark cookie crumbs falling from their giggling mouths. Those crumbs were from *her* chocolate sandwich cookies!

She stuffed her feet into her shoes without bothering to tie them. Nothing was sacred in Ohio. At least before, her dad had understood the sanctity of their chocolate sandwich cookies. Back in Savannah he would have never thought of offering her cookies to little kids who didn't know well enough not to bounce on other people's furniture with their mouths stuffed full of food. She was walking to school.

"You ready to go, Gert?" Her father appeared from nowhere, his coat in his hand. Other fathers called their daughters "Princess," but her dad's term of endearment for her was "Gert." Where the name ever came from was beyond her knowledge, but that's what he called her.

A smile crossed her face as she nodded.

Dads—how can you actually stay mad at them?

He always seemed to know exactly when to mess up one of her perfectly good angry moods. Even at his worst, it was too hard to stay mad for long.

He held the door for her as he called back to his guests to make themselves at home. The laughter was a bit unsettling. Visions of the college sweatshirt trio jumping on her sofa while eating her cookies in their absence crossed her mind. It was her experience that Christian dads tended to be more mischievous than most of their children. Some of the things men back at her home church would pull would land a teenager with a one-way ticket to a night in jail. Of course, her dad was seldom included. He had much more pressing things to do with his time than being part of the men's ministry group—such as teaching the senior women's Bible study. Her dad had little time for fun like most of the "normal" men in her past church.

Man, he's so naive.

Like he really knew any of these people well enough to leave them alone in their house! Those people could be just waiting for the right moment to clean their house out. He really was way too trusting at times.

I suppose he'll learn he can't trust every person who claims to be a "Christian" the day we come home to an empty house.

CHAPTER 11

Why does he have to honk every time he drops me off somewhere?

Now, thanks to dear old dad, Jenna Rose's planned inconspicuous entrance was blown. As the car left the parking lot, again its horn sounded.

Oh, he can be such a dork!

The gathering of guys congregated at the gym doors turned at the blast. Jockish kinds of guys with letterman coats and smelly gym bags, normal haircuts, and Abercrombie clothes turned and looked straight at her. Flashing a smile, she squeezed her way through the middle of them, making sure she brushed slightly against the hip of the best-looking one of the group.

"Who was that?" she heard the cute one ask the rest. A smile spread across her face as she continued across the gym floor to the adjoining gymnastics room where the tryouts were to be held. She liked his tone—for the first time since coming to old Hicksville, someone was showing her the interest she was used to.

"Just haven't made enough of an effort to show your face in the right places, girl," she chided herself. Amy would think she was slipping.

The cute guy was on the varsity baseball team. She knew because his face had recently been plastered all over the front of the sports page for breaking the school's home-run record. There had been a lot of hoopla about the fact that he was still a junior with one whole year of ball left to play. Some commentators said he was well on his way to making big things happen in the game of baseball. Jamie Valentin was his name. In the pictures he looked much taller than he really was. Jenna Rose found that he had maybe an inch or two on her five foot, four, but he was even more muscular than the pictures made him out to be. He had just about the right amount of muscle actually—not that swimmer-kind of lean but not that top-heavy, I-have-no-neck Arnold sort of build either. There wasn't anything particularly striking about his looks. His eyes were light brown and his buzz cut–styled dark hair screamed, "I don't have the time or desire to do anything with my hair other than wash it." If it weren't for the fact that he was a jock, there would be nothing about him that would distinguish him from most of the guys in this school, she surmised truthfully, delighted to hear him coming to find her all the same. Still, he definitely was no Parker. . . .

"Hey," he called as she heard his steps turn into a run. He caught up beside her and tapered the run into a swagger she suspected he had spent years mastering. "Tell me, why don't I know you?"

The sides of her mouth curled slightly as she tried to keep it under control.

That's the best you've got?

Fifth-grade boys at last year's church camp had had better pickup lines than that. "Haven't looked in the right places, I guess," she replied, picking up her pace as she approached the doors. Laughter and muddled tunes from dueling radios greeted her. "I don't know you either."

"Well, where should I start looking?"

"Do I look like I would just give that kind of information out? I'm around. You'll just have to find me, I guess." Too bad her hair wasn't down. This would be the perfect time for a *Charlie's Angels* hair flip. Guys seemed to eat that up from blonds like her. Instead, she gave him her best flirty smile over her shoulder and entered the practice room.

That should be enough to keep him interested.

About twenty other girls waited in the room, with some standing in groups looking completely relaxed and others practicing or stretching individually and looking totally terrified. A girl who had history with her waved, but Jenna Rose opted to find a spot within sight of the door. Finding the right placement on the floor was imperative. If she was going to have an audience, she needed to know that she could make eye contact if she so desired.

Too bad Parker's out slinging slop or something with the youth group. It would be nice to reverse roles here for awhile and let him be the one watching me for a change.

P.K. or not, Jenna Rose could move with the best of them on a dance floor. That would be sure to get his attention.

As the instructor called them to order, everyone fell into place around her.

"Can we say 'eating disorder'?" mumbled a brunette with dull silver barrettes in her hair. She threw a jagged smile in Jenna Rose's direction and nodded toward the instructor for good measure. The woman standing at the front hardly looked like she should be out of high school herself. "I'm Denise," the brunette continued.

Jenna Rose smiled and gave her name in return.

The instructor quickly mentioned something about teaching sophomore English classes and this being her third year as dance-team coach. Denise was right though—this teacher was bone skinny by teenage standards, much less an adult with *years* of experience behind her. In a blur, the instructor introduced the senior members who, consequently, earned the right to spots on the team simply because of their age. She went on to explain that the seniors would be doing the evaluating. As coach, she reserved the final word. And by final word, she meant there would be no negotiating, bargaining, or second chances. She had the power.

There were six spots to fill, but they could accept up to nine new dancers if there was just *that* much talent among the new recruits. Her tone of voice spoke differently though. She should have just screamed, "You guys are all a bunch of losers wasting my time. Get your sorry butts home." There couldn't possibly be anyone out there with an ounce of the talent of her precious seniors.

Low expectations. Good.

All the more chance to wow them and win her rightful place among these peers.

One of the seniors stepped forward. "From this moment on," she began. Given the seriousness in her voice, one would think the world's very balance was hanging on their ability to make a spot on Highland High's summer dance team. "You will be evaluated on how you present yourself, how fast you learn the moves, and if you have what it takes to be a part of this team. Most of you will not be asked to the first practice. Don't feel bad. All you guys are really young and you'll be able to come back in the fall and blow 'em away then if you practice and just believe in yourself. Today we are only looking for the best of the best."

Future motivational speaker material here.

Jenna Rose bent slightly at the waist, trying to keep limber as the girl continued with the game plan for the day. First they were going to learn the basic steps that most high school dance teams used. That part was a cakewalk. Then they were going to be broken down into small groups to learn a routine and basically go head-to-head for the six spots.

As the music began, Jamie and two other guys from the outside group filed into the room.

Ha ha, I sure do still have it.

Sliding a hand into the pocket of his baggy dark blue designer jeans, the baseball star leaned against the wall directly in her line of vision and held her gaze for a moment. With a quick wink, he broke off the look and laughed at something his friend whispered.

He might not be the hunk Parker was, but he definitely had a compelling air about him.

Momentarily she caught his eye, then looked away and smiled sheepishly.

If this boy was game, she would let herself be seen with him some until Parker came to his senses or she got over this crazy crush on the skater boy. Guys that made the front page of the local paper as much as Jamie Valentin did had to have the kind of social standing she was looking for to get where she belonged in this place. If Parker were here, would he have come in to cheer her on like Jamie?

Nah, he'd be out there playing imaginary drums with some pencils or damaging school property with a skateboard.

Jamie the baseball stud was interested in her, and if that was a ticket to getting her into the right set of friends, she was going to make herself be interested right back.

Going through the first part of the tryouts was as easy as Jenna Rose expected it to be. The steps they practiced were pretty basic, and everyone seemed to catch on quickly. Jamie held his spot against the wall while laughing and clumsily mocking their moves. Some of the other girls seemed annoyed by the presence of the boys, but Jenna Rose was enjoying the attention too much to be bothered by their antics.

"Take a ten-minute break," the senior who appeared to be running the show called out at the end of the first section. "We're going to figure out the squads for the second section, and then we'll get back into it."

With a hasty glance over her shoulder to see where her admirer was, Jenna Rose trotted to the drinking fountain. It appeared she was the only one who didn't come equipped with her own bottled water.

They aren't in the twenty-first century as far as their music goes around here, but everyone drinks bottled water. Go figure.

She could take that as her cue to stop drinking the tap water—maybe they all knew something she didn't. Licking at the dribble of lukewarm water on her lip, she decided to go exploring. There was a vending machine in the lobby, or maybe the lunchroom one had bottled water. With all the recent drama about big soda corporations and schools, she'd probably find herself in one of the ones doing away with machines entirely.

Luckily she was in a school that needed money more than morals—three soda vending machines were tucked around the corner between the gym and the lunchroom. Perfect.

She stopped at the first machine and sorted through the change in her hand.

Jamie reached out and pulled her by the arm between two of the machines before she really even saw him there. He held her close to him, his fingers locked together around her waist.

Wow, you smell good.

"Did ya miss me?" he asked.

She really didn't mind his arms being around her waist, but there was something about his fingers locking her in that nerved her out a bit. With no one else around, she didn't particularly like feeling trapped by a guy she had met just thirty minutes ago. "I didn't know I was supposed to," she replied. "Was I? You were in my face the whole time."

"I think you should go out with me," he stated. "This weekend."

"You have plans already tonight?" she asked sarcastically.

"Something like that." His grip relaxed momentarily, giving her the opportunity to squirm free. His hand scooped along her rear as she backed away slightly. No guy had ever touched her there before. She smiled, hoping he caught her uneasiness but still knew she wasn't totally creeped out.

She was caught a bit off guard was all. Talk about moving fast. What was this guy's deal? It was nearly two months since her last good flirt, she told herself. Maybe she was a little out of practice. As she turned to head back to the tryouts, he seized her hand and tried to pull her close again. This time she held her ground.

"You don't have to leave yet," he whispered in her ear, licking his lip slowly. "We can take a few minutes to get to know each other a little better."

Jerking her arm down, she released herself from his grip. Jenna Rose wasn't sure what his definition of "better" was, but something inside told her that staying around to find out might not be a wise choice. "I need to get back to tryouts."

He darted after her again as she turned to walk away. "There's no real hurry yet. They won't even miss you. I just want to get to know you some. I know as well as you do that you were digging on me, so let's just take some time to get to know one another a bit. I don't even know your name."

"I really don't think this is the time," she argued, trying to sidestep his advance.

Instead, he placed his hands low on the sides of her hips as he tried to keep her in front of him. "I can't believe I haven't seen you before. I would know if I had."

A scream welled up in her throat. She choked it back as she reminded herself that he was just talking. Except for invading her personal space a bit, he hadn't really done anything wrong yet.

Pushing past him, she quickened her pace through the gym. "I need to get back to the tryouts," she repeated. A heavy sigh of relief escaped her lips as she waited for the sound of his footsteps and heard none.

Okay, that was not fun.

"Hey," he called after a moment's hesitation. She stopped once again, swallowing the scream that wanted to sound. "I can make or break those tryouts for you. That's your decision."

Oh God. Please tell me he did not just say what he said.

His expensive boots reverberated across the floor as he approached.

He did not just threaten me with making the team. Please tell me he did not.

She could sense him coming closer, but she didn't dare turn around. Her feet were frozen into place. There was fear, anxiety, maybe even a bit of excitement—she wasn't sure what was keeping her there, but she couldn't bring herself to move.

"I don't get turned down in this school," he said and circled around her. "There are girls who would kill to be in your place right now."

Go ask one of them out then.

His hand was on her arm when the girl who had introduced herself as Denise ducked her head out of the gymnastics room. Jenna Rose's insides wanted to crawl away from his touch, but she couldn't bring herself to do it. "Jenna," the girl called, "we're ready to get started again. Let's go. Hi, Jamie."

The sound of Denise's voice snapped Jenna Rose out of her daze.

"Hey, 'Nise," Jamie replied, still keeping his hand on Jenna Rose's arm.

"Break is over," Jenna Rose heard herself mumble from what seemed like a million miles away. "I really need to get back in there."

Hurrying away from him, she dropped her bottled water. The top popped off with a loud bang as she bolted across the floor. Her feet wanted to sprint as fast as they could, not stopping until she was back in Savannah where the guys weren't creeps. Instead, she coolly kept up her pace and headed straight toward Denise.

I don't care. Just get in there.

The sound of water spilling out was almost comforting. She felt like grabbing up the girl who had saved her and burying her face into her shoulder.

Just get your game face on. Get back in there and worry about the task at hand.

Tears were forming.

No, no, no. Don't even start that. Just get in there and do what you came to do. Don't let anyone see you blubbering like a baby. That is not the impression that we are going for here. Stop it.

Somehow she kept the tears at bay as she rejoined the other girls. The instructor tapped her watch, an annoyed look of disgust showing on her face. Jenna Rose nodded and mumbled an apology as she found an open spot on the floor.

God, please let Amy be home tonight. I so need her right now.

"Jenna!" Jamie called out. His voice was once again mixed with the pleasantries he first used when they met at the gym door, a moment that seemed like centuries ago. "Good luck making the team. I'll see you around."

CHAPTER 12

Lunch. The new kid's most dreaded period. There was not a more defining moment in the school day that reminded Jenna Rose she was on new ground than that split second when she turned around with lunch tray in hand and looked about the cafeteria. There was no one anxious for her to come sit down. Nobody. All she saw was a bunch of strange faces not interested in her being at their table.

Here she was almost a month into her new school, but the dreaded lunchroom experience still hadn't changed.

No Jamie Valentin anywhere in sight, thank goodness.

She took another quick scan of the room to see if there was anyone half-interesting to sit by but came up empty.

Faces from the dance tryouts Saturday caught her eye. Those people were her crowd. No one close to best friend material yet, but sitting with them was definitely a step in the right direction. Denise and another girl had an opening at their table on the far side of the room. It looked like her kind of crowd sat back there—girls in designer clothes and jocks with rippling arms were scattered in groups at the tables by the windows. The girls giggled and chatted as they sipped on their diet drinks and watched the guys.

And Jamie Valentin was not among them.

I love your shirt, Denise. That blue looks great on you.

Yeah, that was all she had to say. One quick little icebreaker and they would gladly invite her to sit down. An instant friendship would develop.

This is ridiculous. Why am I so nervous over making friends? I was like the most popular girl in the whole eighth grade last year. Why does it have to be any different here?

Take a deep breath, smile, and go on over there.

Following her advice, Jenna Rose grasped her tray tightly and started toward the two sophomore cheerleaders.

Five steps, four, three...

The blond took one last slurp of her diet drink and got to her feet. Denise, with her cute blue top, followed. They dumped their things in the trashcan and left the lunchroom without even acknowledging her.

Just perfect.

Glancing around now after being this close to the table would be too obvious. If anyone were watching, they would know she had just been dissed.

Just sit your butt down and pray no one saw that. You'll look like you wanted to just have a seat at an empty table. Sit down.

A sigh escaped her lips as she slid her purse from her shoulder and onto the bench. She had a beautiful view of the wall and a poster of some has-been rock star promoting the importance of five-a-day. Of course this pathetic school couldn't have good posters like the "Read" posters in her old school library. If you had to look at a wall to save face, at least you could be looking at Enrique or something.

Another totally wasted lunch.

She dropped her tray down on the table and sat down.

This is food?

A slice of meatloaf that closely resembled a grease-covered brick and smelled about the same slid across her plate. The pears in their spicy sauce wiggled around from the impact. Pushing around some slimy orange-colored potatoes with her fork, she decided the chocolate milk would just have to do for today. Five-a-day, shmive-a-day. Someone should sue for false advertising. Reconstituted potatoes and sugar-covered canned fruit could barely be considered edible, very less healthy food.

"Those are the funkiest looking cheesy potatoes I have ever seen," a voice stated over Jenna Rose's shoulder.

These people love to sneak up on me.

Darby McKennitt stood beside her, a lunch bag in hand. "You'll learn soon enough what days are the best days to bring your own." She shrugged her shoulders and let a grin spread across her face. "Pretty much every day actually. Mind if I sit?"

Jenna Rose shrugged and pointed at the bench.

Why not sit down? It's your school. I can't stop you.

In her estimation, the has-been rock star from the poster would have been a suitable lunch companion.

"So, how do you like Highland?" Darby asked as she swung her legs around and sat down beside her. Jenna Rose had never really known someone with such odd taste in clothes who looked so cute. Her patch-work flair-legged jeans were normal enough, but her red Chucks with scribbled-on soles and black baby doll T-shirt wouldn't quite work on anyone else. But for Darby, it seemed perfect.

With the right look, this girl could be something around here.

Every time Jenna Rose had seen her, her long bangs hung haphaz-ardly in front of her face. Jenna Rose wondered who Darby was hid-ing from.

"Nobody's really given me a chance to make an opinion about this place," she replied, digging around in the potatoes again. The cheese sauce almost had a rubbery consistency. As gross as the orange mound was, the potatoes were fascinating to mess with. She just couldn't help herself from playing around in them.

Darby nodded in understanding and took her lunch from her sack—a granola bar, banana, and small container of peanut butter. "People will be fine once you get to know them. I think change scares them a bit. Give them some time to get to know you, and they'll warm up to you."

Watching with mild interest, Jenna Rose frowned as Darby began to spread the peanut butter on top of the granola bar. Once finished, she peeled the banana and stuck it on top. "I know. I know. I eat weird stuff," she apologized. "It's really good though. I suggest trying it sometime."

Andria plopped down across from them, her lunch bag and can of pop in hand. "You haven't seen the half of it. If she ever ate normal food, I would pass out. Her favorite though, get this, is peanut butter and pickle sandwiches."

Darby chuckled at the face Jenna Rose made in return. "It's really not bad if you try it."

Shanice, clad in a pair of baggy khakis, boots, and a long-sleeved T-shirt that simply said "Christian girl" in little letters, found a seat next to her. Rubbery plastic bracelets of various colors covered her wrists. "Do we have to spend the whole lunch period always talking about the weird things Darby eats?" she piped in, elbowing her friend. Darby lowered her head, trying to hide her reddening face.

Jenna Rose felt a tinge of sorrow for her—she really seemed embarrassed by their jabs. It always made her uncomfortable to see others in distress. "I eat weird stuff too," she stated calmly, trying to turn the conversation away from Darby's food choices.

Please don't ask me what because I can't think of anything right now. And don't ask me why I care either because I don't have a clue myself.

And, of course, they didn't ask.

Andria and Shanice exchanged glances and then hugged Darby at the same time. "I love you, cuz," Shanice barked. Andria just laughed.

The other twin pulled her own lunch out of her sack and turned her attention to Jenna Rose. "So, why didn't you come by for practice last night? Parker made it sound like you wouldn't miss it for anything."

Here goes.

"I tried out for dance team last night."

"Did you make it?" Darby asked, excitement sounding in her voice.

"I'll know soon, I guess." She caught sight of one of the guys with Jamie at the tryouts, but he was alone. She doubted the baseball player would give her any trouble after she dismissed him, but she honestly didn't look forward to finding out how he would react.

Shanice hopped up and down in her seat excitedly. "Oh, I so told you we could be a pop band! See? We'd do the dance steps ourselves. We could so do it."

"The only dancing I'll do will be from my stool," Darby retorted, tossing her hair from her face in false snobbishness. Her bangs instantly landed back in her eyes. "I'm a musician. No dancing."

Walking around the table and squeezing in beside her, Shanice placed her arms around both Jenna Rose and Darby. "We'll just dance circles around you, Miss Somber and Serious," she said to Darby. "We can have some fun once in awhile. It says 'make a *joyful* noise unto the Lord' you know."

Oh, here we go. I am not spending my lunch at a Bible study. No thank you. What am I doing? I need to get moving. . . . I have fifteen minutes of lunch left, and here I am talking to myself.

It was getting a bit nerve-wracking that the most intelligent conversations she was having since moving to Ohio were with herself.

Maybe you can find Denise and see what she's doing for the rest of the time.

"You guys have a good lunch," Jenna Rose said abruptly as she stood up. Shanice's arm fell limply off of her. "I've got things I need to get done. I just remembered."

Dumping her things in the trash, she looked back to see them whispering among themselves. Darby caught her eye and gave a weak smile.

Great. Now she's going to think I want to be her best friend or something just because I stood up for her. Sorry. Gotta be social suicide to hang out with a bunch of Bible beater skater freaks. Even in this school. Have a good life. See ya! I don't see us becoming friends anytime soon, dearie. So keep on whispering.

Her locker was just around the corner from the lunchroom. She'd stop there, grab her books for her next class, and then track down Denise and the other girl to see if they knew anything about the results of the tryouts. That was a safe way to make an approach.

As she rounded the corner, she noticed a piece of paper protruding from the vents of her locker. Must be some mistake. Curious, she surveyed the hallway for the person who left the note. It had to be for someone else—she didn't really know anyone other than the people she just sat with at lunch, and they wouldn't leave her a note when she was just with them. No one was around. She pulled the neatly folded computer paper from her locker.

The note had her name written on the outside. It was for her. Inside, it simply said, "Guess who didn't make the team?"

CHAPTER 13

Why she was there, she had no idea. No, actually she did. Jenna Rose knew exactly why she was there. Parker expected her. He wanted her there, they said. And how could she resist? Their paths never crossed in school save for a few minutes spent on the bus and during a monster study hall with him sitting clear on the other side of the auditorium. He probably didn't even notice her sneaking glances his way while she pretended to read her social studies book. Half the kids in school had to be in that study hall.

She was pretty clueless about why she was following him around so much. Parker was so different than any other guy she ever liked. . . and he didn't even seem interested in dating. He didn't seem to have a clue. Chasing a guy couldn't possibly take this much work all the time. This was all new territory to her. If anything, she was used to being the one who was chased. Like this whole Jamie thing but not so psycho. That whole thing was just nuts.

Yet here she was.

She sipped on her drink and focused on the two Angelinos bustling around the kitchen. To watch them, one would think they had a hundred orders to fill. They moved quickly and efficiently, and it was obvious they took great pride in their work. Jenna Rose was sure though that when it was closing time, they didn't think any more about pizza until the doors opened the next day. Unlike her dad, of course. Too bad her dad couldn't learn from them. He lived, ate, and breathed his job.

Playing with a fuzzy on the sleeve of her red sweater, she wondered about what kind of clothes Parker was into when it came to girls. Jenna Rose had gone through her closet a hundred times trying to find just the right thing. This red sweater with its mock turtleneck was soft and comfy with just the right level of modesty. He could forget about her dressing like some skater chick—it wasn't going to happen. Her stonewashed jeans with rhinestones running down the flared legs were about as crazy as her wardrobe could be.

But maybe that was part of it. Maybe she didn't have the look for him. *This is probably a gag.*

They were probably all hiding with half the school and laughing at her right now because she showed up. Some pathetic *Carrie*-like prank or something similar on the new P.K. in town. She imagined Parker and Jamie with their arms slung around each other's shoulders and mimicking her every move. Maybe that's what they did for fun around here—play pranks on the new kids in school. They were probably all rolling around on the frozen ground in laughter at her expense. Yet she was still sitting here taking it.

Jenna Rose glanced at her watch and then back out the window. No one was lurking in the bushes by the bank across the street. Not Parker and his pals or Jamie either. If they were laughing at her expense, they were doing a good job of hiding.

As she swirled her straw in circles, her thoughts drifted back to school that day. She had checked the board in the gymnasium before boarding the bus for some clue to whether she made the team, but nothing had been posted. The neatly written note from her locker gradually ate away at her confidence, even though she knew she had done as well as any other girl in that tryout, if not better. Her usual sureness about her abilities had been replaced with a few simple words—"I can make or break this tryout for you."

Did he really know if she didn't make it? Did he have some inside track on who was named to the team? Or did he really keep her off the team because she wouldn't willingly give in to his advances as he had implied?

The instructor had said it might take a day or two to get the results posted. Jenna Rose wanted to believe Jamie was only bluffing and that he didn't have that kind of clout. Yet deep down she had a feeling. Even in her old hometown of Savannah, the sports stars regularly gracing the cover of the local papers usually did have that kind of clout.

She glanced again at her watch and stared out the wide window into the parking lot.

This was supposed to be *their* hangout place. So why weren't they here?

Elijah and Andria suddenly bounded across the parking lot. Hand in hand, they bounced as they walked, laughing over something that must have been incredibly funny. Amber, her reddish hair in a ponytail, followed them through the entrance. She smiled and gestured at Jenna Rose to go with them into the back room. Dropping her eyes to her glass, Jenna Rose acted like she didn't notice. She stared into her straw and pretended to count the bubbles rising to the surface while memorizing the color of the cola—anything that would get her out of following them into that room. If Parker didn't show up, she wasn't hanging around. It would be easier to take off if she stayed out here.

Darby came through the door next. Her hands were pulled up in the sleeves of her oversized hoodie. Her face was red much like Jenna Rose's had been when she got here. "They must not live far away if they're able to walk here as well," she mumbled to herself.

Come on. Do you really care?

She pushed the thought from her mind. If it weren't for Parker, she wouldn't even associate with these people.

Elijah popped his head out of the door. "Jenna? You coming?"

Undecided, she glanced back through the big picture windows. She really wasn't interested in staying around if Parker wouldn't be here. Singing with them was fun enough, but to stay on purpose without him? There was no point to it.

"Oh, he's on his way," the boy urged in a hurried tone. "Come on. Let's get some vocal work done while we wait."

It *was* nice to have the chance to sing. Standing up slowly, she searched her mind for some excuse to just go home without sounding stupid.

Yeah, I just came clear down here to get a Coke. Really, it had nothing to do with your cute guitarist or the fact that this is the place you play. Forget about the fact that there's a drive-in place a half a block from my house. You can't get a drink with ice at those places. Yeah, that's it. Coming here had nothing to do with him. Really it didn't.

Nothing sounded good enough. Admitting defeat to herself, she pushed in her chair and followed.

Unlike the first time she entered the room, two windows now let in light, which made the room seem much less mysterious. It now resembled the dusty old storage room that it really was. She kind of missed the mystique. It was much more romantic and fitting to a *Rockumentary* set that way—she had liked the atmosphere.

Was the smell of old cardboard here last time?

Parker didn't seem to be that interested in making it big when he described their vision for the group. He didn't want to be a coffeehouse band, but he didn't want to be splashed all over MTV. So what was he looking for? There really wasn't an in-between the way Jenna Rose saw it. You either made it or you didn't. Could there really be something else to it?

Darby was already perched on her stool, studying her fingers carefully as she played with a new chord. Jenna Rose smiled slightly at her. She had a feeling Darby wouldn't ever leave that stool if they would just let her stay there. Her fingers danced so effortlessly across the strings. The girl really was very talented on the guitar—an instrument Jenna Rose had at one time been interested in taking up after seeing a performer. That was back when church camp was the highlight of her year. Soon after, someone had commented on her vocal abilities, and, well, the rest was history. People with her kind of talent didn't need to play an instrument to make it. That's what studio musicians were for. But Darby really was good, and she seemed to enjoy it.

On the other side of the room, Andria sat backwards in a chair, poring over some music. She twirled one drumstick in her hand, tapping her foot to the rhythm on the paper. What a tomboy this chick was.

I bet she even knows how to do that ollie skateboard trick.

Andria's blue velour-looking retro sweat suit had to be the ugliest clothing Jenna Rose had ever seen. On her head was a red-white-and-blue sweatband, though her red hair was still sticking up wildly in all directions. She looked like one of the ad models from a magazine Amy and Jenna Rose had tossed at each other while joking over who would receive such an outfit as a crank Christmas gift. Who knew people actually bought those sorry clothes?

The only halfway normal-looking one of the bunch was Amber, who was already hidden behind her mixing board. She was fumbling with some wires and had her headphones on. Amber hadn't spoken a word to Jenna Rose yet, but she seemed like a pleasant enough person. One of those girls you were glad to sit by in study hall because she was interesting enough to talk to, though not interesting enough to hang with on a Friday night. Her sweater was a solid purple cable knit and her leggings were black, comfortable-looking cotton. Not cover material for *YM* magazine, but normal enough.

Unlike Elijah, who looks like he stepped off the cover of What-Was-I-Thinking *magazine.*

His blue plaid pants were old-school punk tight and just a bit short in length. He had coupled the pants with a form-fitting black T-shirt, red skater shoes—*are those the same shoes Andria was wearing just yesterday? Gross!*—and a knee-length black coat. Jenna Rose wished she had a class or two with this guy just to see what people at school had thought of his outfit. She'd never seen anything like it.

Those couldn't be the same shoes. He has to have bigger feet than she! Would they really coordinate their shoes. . . ? Weirdos.

Her legs wanted to turn and run. The phrase "Save yourself while you're still normal" ran through her head, urging her legs to stand up and make an exit quickly. She should get away from these people and go find someone else to hang out with who wasn't so weird. Even spaghetti-arms Jamie was normal. She even turned and looked at the entrance, contemplating if she should make some lame excuse or just bolt.

And then Parker walked in the door.

Parker with the bouncy perfect-curls hair, piercing eyes, and electric smile.

He came in the door and placed his guitar case by the drums, laughing and shaking his head though his gaze never left Elijah. "Bro, what is that?" he gasped in a breath.

"What?" The bassist threw his arms open, his instrument hanging from its bright green strap. The grin on his face declared that his outfit had been the subject of many conversations that day, but also that he had wanted nothing less.

"I so never expected you to really get them! Wow. They are you! Just a bit weird and over the top."

Andria's eyes never left the music sheet in her hand as she retorted, "Hey, I happen to like the pants!"

Parker started laughing harder. "Oh, that's even better! Now I know why you have the pants. The little woman has spoken. Girlfriend likes them so we must have them, right?" Covering his head, he ducked as a drumstick went flying past. "You're taking this rock-star thing too seriously, dude."

Elijah shrugged his shoulders and adjusted his guitar strap. "Hey, it works for K-Max."

"I guess every band has to have a freak."

"Man, if this band wasn't your thing, I'd kick you out for being late again," Elijah mumbled, a playful smile lighting his face.

Parker took his guitar from the case and plugged it into his amplifier. "Yeah, yeah. Sometimes things happen. Now let's play."

CHAPPTER 114

Resting a hand flat on her stomach, Jenna Rose took a deep breath. Her belly was doing flip-flops! Parker hadn't spoken a word to her since he arrived, and here they were about to start into their second song. Actually, he hadn't even looked her way. Did he really want her there? Maybe he didn't. Maybe this was just more of some elaborate hoax. Some let's-see-how-many-days-she'll-come-here-thinking-she's-going-to-be-accepted kind of thing.

Well, she had news for them. She wasn't going to take part in their hazing because she didn't want to be part of their crowd. She *wasn't* part of their crowd. She belonged with normal kids who liked dating and football games and shopping at the mall—the kinds of things kids her age were supposed to be doing. The whole save-the-world Christian punk skater thing and new-age hippie stuff wasn't for her.

Something told her that Parker should be in her kind of crowd too. Deep down in his gut, he had to know it. He just needed the right encouragement to get him there. He was a lost soul, and she would make it her mission to get him back on the right track. So he skated. Elijah said the trick Parker performed for her was a simple one anyone could learn. Who's to say that he'd been skating for that long?

An urge to jump up and just interrupt their playing came over her. That's what she would do: Just step right up and say, "Look, I like you. I think we should be together."

What would it really hurt? She'd get her answer, wouldn't she? So they would miss a few minutes of their practice. Really, what were they practicing for? They weren't looking for any gigs or anything as far as she could tell. No big shows loomed in the near future. What would just a few minutes hurt? She would just get to her feet and ask him the question.

But will I like his answer?

That simple little thought kept her firmly planted in her seat. There was no way she could bring herself to get up and try it for fear of what might happen, which made her mad.

Why would he reject her?

Why wouldn't he want to be with her? Back home, guys were probably still lined up to be with her. Every guy had wanted to date her. She couldn't keep up with all the guys who wanted to go out with her. There was nothing *that* special about Parker. He was no different than any of the rest of them.

But it didn't matter. She was frozen in place. He would be the one doing the asking. She just had to step up the signals a bit. Maybe he was confusing them with something else. Maybe he was under the impression that she wasn't allowed to date with her dad being, well, himself. Something was up. . .though obviously he was noticing something or he wouldn't still be around.

The band had been working on music for almost forty-five minutes. Parker stopped occasionally and barked orders at the others, and each suggestion made the next take even better. Jenna Rose was impressed. He really did know what he was doing.

Shanice sat on the far side of the room studying a music sheet Darby had handed her. With large, clunky headphones that made her head look out of proportion with the rest of her body, Amber danced to the music and simultaneously twisted knobs and pushed buttons at Parker's command.

Darby had pulled her hair back into a ponytail, and for the first time Jenna Rose could see her entire face. She was bent over her guitar, eyes closed as she played.

She needs to keep her hair out of her eyes more often. She's really pretty.

Her twin sister had shed her sweatshirt to reveal only a white tank top. Jenna Rose shivered at the sight of her—it was rather chilly in this room.

Drummers must really work up a sweat because you always see them stripped down, sometimes too far. Either that or they have a natural tendency to be exhibitionists.

Jenna Rose had sat in her chair the whole time and felt very much like a starstruck groupie instead of part of the band. So maybe she wasn't part of the band *officially* yet—not that she wanted to be either. Every P.K. in the world knew the songs they were singing. She could just jump in and start singing quite easily. Shanice was good enough, though a bit nasally at times and definitely a little too into the hip-hop influence with her fluctuating notes and little added extras. Jenna Rose was confident she could bust these songs out like they had never heard if they would just give her the chance.

That's why they all like me around. I make them feel like a real band or something.

She floated into a daydream for awhile, thinking about that day when she would be a pop diva. Life would be good then.

They were done playing. And Parker was walking straight for her. Come to think of it, they all were. Parker sat down in the chair next to her and then pulled it closer. Tingles flew up her back as his elbow rested against her forearm for a brief moment. Andria crumpled down in front of them cross-legged on the floor, while Elijah relaxed next to her and laid his head on Andria's leg. The others formed a circle around Jenna Rose with their chairs.

Parker smiled at her and wrapped an arm around her shoulder. She gasped in a breath and held it. If her lungs were empty, there would be nothing left inside to keep her from melting away from his touch. Gotta hold that breath. Guys were not supposed to have such soft, perfect skin. He held her gaze for a moment, then winked. Jenna Rose noticed that one of his bottom front teeth was a slight shade darker than the rest, but it hardly detracted from his heartwarming grin.

Okay, so everyone has to have one little flaw.

"I think it's time for us to start striving for the next level," Parker finally broke the silence and stated matter-of-factly.

With his arm still around Jenna Rose's shoulder, he raised a foot and propped it on Elijah's knee. The newcomer to their little clan wondered how long they had all known each other. They seemed so comfortable and familiar with one another. Once upon a time, she had that too— friendship that was so deep and real that words didn't have to be shared to make a moment memorable. But, alas, no more.

"I can really feel the Lord talking to me about this, guys, and He says we're ready."

Jenna Rose bit her lip to keep the groan from escaping. If not for the fact that he was touching her, she would be out the door.

Sheesh, if a voice in your head said to bludgeon your mom to death with a turkey baster, would you say that was God too?

People who blamed and credited God for everything just got under her skin. Like God doesn't have something better to do than worry about the success of a little teenage garage band from Nowhere, Ohio?

Parker. . .why do you have to be so perfect but at the same time so not?

Parker continued, "You want to take over, 'Lijah?"

Elijah nodded as he sat up. "I got news." He paused for dramatic effect. Everyone leaned closer waiting for his next words. "I got us a couple gigs. The first one is just kinda a practice one over at Central Baptist. The big one is a four-set opening at the Youth for Christ convention up in Akron."

Count me out. Don't think I'm going off to some church to yell "amen" and talk about all the wonderful ways God has changed my life. Still waiting for it to happen. Not going to happen, I'm betting.

Instant chatter erupted. Holding up his hand, Elijah gestured for silence as he continued. "I know a guy from there who's starting up an Indy label. He's willing to help us get a demo, maybe even a whole CD if we're ready. I think we are."

Parker nodded in agreement.

"Isn't that expensive?" Amber asked.

Big surprise that she would be the sensible one.

"He's willing to do the demo for forty bucks an hour. That's a real steal. Between these two gigs, if we can make a few hundred bucks, we should have it covered. Plus, I've got some cash. Anyone else?" He looked around the room, studying each person's face slowly.

"I don't have much," Andria stated, "but what I do have is all yours."

Her sister nodded. "Same here. But I'm thinking we ought to have the demo done before the big gig. Wouldn't it be sweet to have some copies available for sale?"

"And we could put it on the Internet," Andria interjected.

A smile spread across Elijah's face. "Yeah, we definitely need a site with some MP3 downloads available."

"We need some of Darby's stuff on this CD too," Parker added, giving his friend a wink. "Some of our own original stuff and not just covers."

Darby shook her head and slumped back in her seat. "I don't think any of my stuff is good enough. Not for a real CD anyway. . .no way. I don't want to be the one that holds us back before we even get started."

"Too bad," Parker said in reply. "You're our songwriter."

"And a darned good one too," Elijah added.

Parker continued, "Yeah, and we will be using your stuff."

The other girls also agreed. All eyes turned to Jenna Rose. Parker's arm was still around her, and it felt so good. Her smile seemed to be a good enough response for them—they turned their gaze back toward Elijah.

"Wait a minute," Andria stated as her boyfriend returned his head to his resting spot on her lap. "How can we be booked somewhere when we don't even have a name?"

The two guys exchanged grins. Parker rested his head in the palms of his hands.

Elijah sat up again. "Well, we do have a temporary name. At least until we come up with something we can all agree on."

"What?" Shanice spoke up for the first time. "You named *our* band without the rest of us?"

"No, I said it was just temporary. Flyers are already being made for the Baptist church show, but we can change the name before we even make the convention."

"No," she replied, shaking her head and folding her arms over her chest in disbelief that he would do such a thing.

"What is it?" asked Andria.

"As if you don't know," Shanice barked back.

"I don't know," Andria snapped. "But I think we need to give him the chance to talk before we go throwing out the idea."

"Well, he's your boo," Shanice mumbled, sitting back in the chair. The two looked at one another and then started laughing.

"And if you don't like it, you can just booger off," Andria retorted as she playfully kicked her friend's leg.

Shanice returned her kick more forcefully.

"Hey, now, I didn't hurt you!"

Jenna Rose observed them with mild interest, once again longing for her friend. Amy and she did the same thing—start to fight and then realize how silly they sounded. It always ended with laughter.

I suppose all true friends have that kind of relationship.

"So what is it?" Darby interrupted.

Again, Parker and Elijah looked at one another. Then their heads turned toward Jenna Rose.

They did.

"You didn't!" she exclaimed.

"Well," Elijah answered, ignoring her outburst, "thanks to a recent intellectual conversation that Parker and I were engaged in, we came up with a temporary name."

"I don't really like it," Parker interrupted. "I think it'll work until we come up with something else. But I don't think it's serious enough for what we want to accomplish.

"Anyway, we were informed in this conversation that Christian music was just copying mainstream music. This person went so far as to suggest that Christian musicians were second rate."

Jenna Rose just glared at him.

"So with much deliberation, I give you Second Rate," Elijah announced.

Parker then jumped in, a piece of paper in hand. "We'll say our name comes from the fact that most music fans think Christian music isn't very good. Matthew 19:28–30 says, 'Jesus said to them, "I tell you the truth, at the renewal of all things, when the Son of Man sits on his glorious throne, you who have followed me will also sit on twelve thrones, judging the twelve tribes of Israel. And everyone who has left houses or brothers or sisters or father or mother or children or fields for my sake will receive a hundred times as much and will inherit eternal life. But many who are first will be last, and many who are last will be first." ' We may be second-rate musicians today to the world, but someday we'll be first in the kingdom of God."

Oh, barf, barf.

"That was impressive, Parker," Shanice stated, her tone of voice clearly saying she wasn't really very impressed at all. "But I don't want to be in a band called Second Rate. It's corny. Even with your biblical explanation, which was cool, it's still corny."

"Well, we don't have much of a choice now on the first one," Elijah reminded her. "Flyers are at the press as we speak."

"And another thing," Parker added. "We're going to need some photos. Some band shots for future flyers and stuff. We can get them done, but that's more money that we'll need to make before then. The convention is in June, so we've got a month to go."

"Or we can find someone who takes good pictures," Elijah interrupted. "We can get this done ourselves."

Andria suggested a cousin whom she remembered always took pictures at their summer family reunions and other events. Her sister quickly supported her. Everyone agreed that contacting him should be the first step.

Holding his hands out palms up, Parker stated seriously, "Then I guess Second Rate is all set." Darby grabbed his hand and the others followed. The circle was complete save one spot. Parker held his hand out to the hesitant newcomer.

"Jenna?"

By the time she realized he was there, it was too late to find cover. Jamie Valentin came from behind her with two of his jock cronies when she was halfway up the middle flight of stairs. There was no place to go except the last set of stairs and her class. Her mind was in a whirlwind of panic as he brushed closely against her.

Just keep moving. Get to class.

Taking the steps two at a time, she was quickly surrounded on both sides by the cronies. Their eyes looked straight ahead like they were just climbing a busy staircase to class. But the staircase wasn't busy. Only a couple classrooms were on the top floor—some science labs and the band room, and not many students needed to be up there at that time. She had never seen him in this hallway between these periods before, so obviously this diversion was for her benefit.

I will not panic.

Jamie climbed the stairs directly behind her so his body could touch hers as they walked. His woodsy cologne filled her nose as a sickening feeling swept over her at its smell. Once upon a time, she had loved that scent—she had even taken sample cards from the mall boutiques and tucked them away into her journal to daydream over as she wrote.

Never again.

"So," he whispered, using that sweet tone dripping with malice that he had used after not getting his way before. She could feel his breath on

86

the back of her neck as he spoke again. "Heard anything from the try-outs yet?"

Jenna Rose closed her eyes and took in a deep breath. Had he really messed up the tryouts for her? She still didn't know if she had made the team or not. Here it was Tuesday, a whole three days later, and she hadn't heard anything. Could he really have sabotaged it for her? Or was he just trying to use it to his advantage?

For a moment, it seemed like the crony closest to the banister was going to tumble over in laughter. The urge to help him fall over was strong, but Jenna Rose resisted. Just a quick readjustment to her over-the-shoulder messenger bag could probably have toppled him.

The other one, a blond with a haircut that closely resembled a mul-let, high-fived Jamie in response.

How can somebody with a mullet be in the "in" crowd, and I can't get any-one to even say hi back to me? Other than Jamie Valentin.

Just keep going. Don't even acknowledge his presence. Don't give him the satisfaction.

Drawing in a deep breath and closing her eyes, she shuddered as his nose touched her ear.

Just think. Only a few days ago, you were attracted to this creep.

"Given any thought as to what we're doing on our date yet?" he asked. "I know I have."

As her feet came to the hallway, she bolted for the first door she saw and closed it quickly behind her.

The crony who almost took a fall waved. "Bye, Jenna," he sang as the trio continued down the hall.

She banged her head in frustration against the steel door as she watched through the small window as they laughed at her. They headed toward the other set of stairs. The hall was virtually empty save a few straggling couples eager to get their last few moments together.

Why was she doing this to herself? Just three days ago, she was toy-ing with the guy and had been interested in making it more than casual flirting. Now she was running from him like he was some stalker. Jamie

Valentin was one of the most popular guys in school—a guy that could probably date any girl he wanted to, and she was making him out to be a monster. This guy could get her into the circles she was striking out in on her own. She wanted his attention, but now that she had it, she was all panicky and acting like she didn't know what to do with it.

Yeah, but he has no business getting that close.

There was a difference between being too close and annihilating someone's personal space. Jamie Valentin was showing no regard for the latter. It creeped her out and made her feel sleazy all at the same time.

She had entered the band room, a vast space with smaller rooms coming off of it. Risers took up one half of the room, while chairs set for the concert band were arranged in the other half. The space seemed empty other than two people sitting back in one of the smaller rooms. The door to the small room was closed, but Jenna Rose could hear music.

Oh great. You're being sexually harassed by the school bully and you run into the big empty room with lots of little hiding places. Real smart, Jenna Rose. . .straight-out-of-a-bad-horror-movie stupid.

The bell sounding made her jump. Now she was late along with everything else. Jenna Rose stretched to see out the tiny window. No way was she going back out there without knowing the way was clear. Mullet Boy stood against a locker catty-corner to the music room door. Darting back out of sight, Jenna Rose mumbled, "Why isn't he in class?"

"That's a very good question," a voice of authority boomed from behind her. "I was about to ask you the same thing."

Fantastic. Add detention to my list of firsts since moving here.

She turned slowly to face a man in his late twenties with his arms full of chorus books. Green eyes showed out from under his gold wire-framed glasses. He looked very *GQ*-casual in his cream knit sweater, baggy tan cords, and Doc Martens. Under normal circumstances, Jenna Rose would have had a crush on him instantly. This time her mind had more important things to worry about.

His expression lightened as he saw the frightened look on her face. "Are you okay?"

She grasped her messenger bag tightly to her chest and tried to look as nervous and lost as possible. "I can't find my class. I got all turned around and lost." The door where the music had come from opened up and two figures emerged. One was Darby McKennitt. She waved excitedly when she saw Jenna Rose.

"I'm new here," Jenna Rose interjected as she returned the wave. He didn't need to know that she had been attending for a few weeks now—technically, she was still new. Hopefully Darby wouldn't blow that for her.

"This place can be a bit confusing at times," he admitted, his face telling her he didn't believe a word of what she had just said. "What class are you looking for?"

Jenna Rose sighed, relieved that even though he suspected more, he wasn't going to push her for it. This was her kind of teacher. "Bio," she replied, knowing full well that her class was just by the other stairs. Probably only four doors down the hallway.

Darby trotted across the risers with her guitar in hand. "Mr. Scott," she called, "this is the friend I was telling you about."

Jenna Rose was surprised to find that she didn't even have the energy to argue with Darby in her head. Let Darby think she was a friend if it kept her out of detention.

Darby dropped her guitar case and swung an arm around Jenna Rose's shoulder. "This is Jenna Rose."

"The one with the voice?" he asked.

Please. How many other Jenna Rose's are there in this school?

Well, if there was more than one, it was nice to know she was "the one with the voice." It was always comforting to know that knowledge of her voice preceded her.

He contorted his face as he rubbed his chin, thinking. "I'll make a deal with you," he stated, dropping the books into a nearby chair and grabbing a hall pass. Jenna Rose hated the sound of the word "deal" coming out of the mouths of teachers. They never meant anything good on her part, but she was willing to listen this time to get herself out of trouble. Anything would be better than explaining to her dad that she had detention for being late to class because she was being harassed by the guy she had been flirting with. *Talk about being grounded until you are thirty.*

"How many study halls do you have?"

"Two," she replied, trying not to laugh at Darby, who was about to burst with excitement behind him. The girl was such a goof. Why did she have to be so annoying yet so darn infectious at the same time?

"I can't get you into honors choir in the middle of the year—school's rules, not mine. But, if you promise to change your schedule around to get in here for some private voice lessons with Miss Inglewood, our voice coach, I'll write you a pass to get you back into class. Of course, you're always welcome to join the chorus, our regular choir program. You'd make a great addition," Mr. Scott finished.

Jenna Rose nodded. Private lessons, she could do. Joining a general choir where any screeching goose could come in thinking she had talent was not a possibility. She may not have found her place in the social standings yet around here, but joining the general choir program was definitely not going to win her points to the top.

Mullet Boy walked past the window and peered in.

Why wasn't anyone hounding him about not being in class?

He strolled past in the other direction.

As Mr. Scott handed her the pass, he noted the change in her complexion. "Darby," he said quietly, his eyes following Jenna Rose's gaze toward the door. Her stalker was nowhere to be seen. "Please escort Ms. Brinley back to her classroom so she doesn't get lost again."

His weak smile said he knew there was more to the story but he would let it go this time. In his eyes she saw a clear-cut message, however: *Bust into my room scared to death again, and I will roll heads getting to the bottom of this.* She was sure it wouldn't come to that. Yeah, she was going to like this Mr. Scott.

Again, she nodded. Part of her wanted to just start talking and let every last thought spill out from the moment her dad told her they were moving until the second she closed the band room door behind her. She refrained. She didn't know this teacher well enough yet to start saying too much. Plus, did she really have hours to talk to him?

Watching for Mullet Boy, she saw that the hall was clear. If she could just get to her last class and then home afterward, this whole mess would be over. By tomorrow, he was sure to have found someone else he was interested in. Now to get to class. . .

Darby walked silently beside her, sending quick glances her way.

Just don't say anything to me and get me to my class.

Everything would be fine if she didn't have to speak as they walked the twenty steps to her classroom.

Then Darby stopped walking. "Jenna, what's goin' on?" she asked.

Tears trickled from Jenna Rose's eyes. She battled them fiercely, trying to fight off their escape. It was bad enough that she had to walk into class late and have everyone look at her, but now she was going to have to do it with puffy, red eyes and mascara running down her face.

Thanks a lot, Darby.

As a sob escaped, she hurried into the rest room.

She wasn't sure what she was going to prove by running into the bathroom to hide. Darby obviously knew where she was. Fleeing to the back stall, she slammed the door closed as the tears started to pour down her face. The bang echoed through the long corridor lined with stalls and sinks, bringing a touch of satisfaction to Jenna Rose. A childish little voice in her head told her to do it again, but she denied it. She found a seat on the closed toilet and then pulled her legs up for good measure. Even though Darby knew where she went, Jenna Rose found comfort in knowing that she wouldn't be found by a quick glance under the doors.

Her head thumped down on her knee as she heard the door open. Miss Goodie-Two-Shoes had followed her in. Why wouldn't this girl leave her alone?

"Jenna, I don't know what's going on," Darby stated as she stopped outside the stall door. "But I want you to know that I'm here for you. I've been told that I'm a really good listener. Whatever it is, let me help you out."

"Go away," Jenna Rose whispered.

"I don't know why you won't let me in."

Because I'm in the bathroom, ew.

She had to fight back a smile over that thought. Amy would have said it. But Jenna Rose couldn't bring herself to say such things. She hated being unkind to people. Why did Darby have to insist on getting in her face and provoking her like this?

"All of us have tried to be your friend, and you just keep shutting us out," Darby began.

"Please," Jenna Rose whispered as she wiped her tears on the knee of her jeans. Black streaks from her mascara smeared across the denim. "Just go away."

"I have tried over and over again to make you realize that I would like to be your friend," Darby continued.

Jenna Rose flung the door open, feeling childishly satisfied as it banged noisily off the bathroom wall. She faced the taller girl standing as straight as she could; she was still three inches shorter. A mixture of anger and fear flowed through her as she cut Darby off: "Yeah, nobody asked you to."

For a fleeting moment, she witnessed Darby's mouth drop in surprise. With a huff, Jenna Rose again slammed the stall door closed and locked it. She pressed her eyes closed and listened for the sound of the door closing. There was nothing.

It must not have made any noise.

Jenna Rose glanced under the stall door—no one was there. And here she was, all alone just like she wanted to be. And feeling more terrible than she ever had before.

The minutes became an hour as she sat and sobbed, glancing now and then to her watch. It had to be time to head home. *Why won't that stupid bell ring?*

She just wanted to go home, crawl into bed, and curse God for letting her dad take her away from her home.

God.

Like He really existed. If God was worth serving like her father faithfully did, then why would He let her have everything and then just rip it out from under her like that? She was convinced her father didn't serve anyone but self-righteous, needy people who expected his care under the guise of loving and serving God. Her mom had also talked about "loving God," but what kind of love could this truly be? As the bell rang signaling the end of the day, Jenna Rose wiped her eyes and unlocked the stall door.

There's no such thing as a loving God.

As she opened the door, she was startled to see Darby sitting on the sink counter with her legs folded underneath her. Jenna Rose gave her a dry but thankful smile as she headed for the door. Darby joined her silently as they made their way to their lockers.

Words wouldn't form in her head or mouth. Darby's just being there spoke volumes—more than any words ever could.

Jenna Rose tossed her books into her locker and grabbed her jacket. There was some homework that she should be taking with her, but she couldn't remember what it could be at the moment. Right now, just getting home was all her head could come up with. Darby stood with her back against the locker beside Jenna Rose, her books clutched tightly against her chest. Her gaze would shift from the wall to Jenna Rose as she waited for some clue as to what was going on.

"You didn't have to hang around like that," Jenna Rose said. She felt like something needed to be said. The words sounded hollow and insincere.

"Yeah, I did," Darby replied.

Jenna Rose closed the locker and flung her bag across her shoulder as she turned to the taller girl. "Well, thanks. I just don't quite get why."

The two started toward the double doors that led to the buses. Scanning the courtyard for Jamie or one of his henchmen, Jenna Rose stepped through the door. Two girls stood outside giggling before hurrying back into the building. The way the one had looked at Jenna Rose pierced her nerves once again. Whatever they were laughing about, Jenna Rose was certain it had something to do with her.

"I've always gone to this school," Darby explained, "and I guess I'm a people-watcher. I like to just observe. I've seen new kids struggle, and I just want to help out. I think you're cool, Jenna, and I think we could be friends. We all need those—especially when we're in new territory when we don't want to be there." Darby pointed to the bus at the front of the line. "I'll see you later, okay?"

Jenna Rose nodded, unsure of what she needed to say. As Darby jogged toward her bus, Jenna Rose bit her bottom lip and watched her. It was getting more difficult every day not to like that girl.

CHAPTER 16

Her heart launching into her throat, Jenna Rose stepped on the bus and noticed it was empty. She swallowed, trying to push it back into place as she gingerly walked down the aisle. Her pulse raced. Jamie seemed to wait for those moments when he could catch her alone.

This is nuts. He has no reason to be on this bus.

"And he had no reason to be by the soda machine the other day or on the stairs today," she told herself out loud. None of whatever it was he was trying to prove made sense. Expecting him to pop up like some B-rated slasher movie from under the seats, she scanned as far in front of her as she could before settling down in the fourth row opposite the driver's seat.

You really need a life. And you need to lay off the horror movies.

Snuggling up against the window, she watched the students as they poured from the building. Maybe just one view of Parker would make everything seem right again. He usually was one of the last people to come on the bus. He would sprint from the building just as the bus driver closed the door. That's what she would do—watch for Parker and pretend like today never happened. The bus started to sway and bounce as other students climbed the steps and found seats.

Two guys heading toward her bus caught her attention. A month on the bus had taught her which faces belonged there and which ones didn't, and she had never seen these two before. Neither one was an eyesore.

She would have noticed them before, cute as they were. They were heading straight for her window. She closed her eyes, willing this to be yet another example of her imagination running wild.

Bam, bam. The heavier one in the hip-length black leather coat pounded on her window. She jumped. He smiled and waved, then made a suggestive gesture with his hand toward his groin. Jenna Rose looked away quickly as they erupted into laughter.

Seems like the idiots come in pairs around here.

A couple boys from the back of the bus snickered. Obviously their attention was for her benefit as well.

She desperately needed something to do without *looking* like she was doing something on purpose. Scanning through her messenger bag, her hand rested on the fuzzy Bible cover. It was soft like the underside down of a baby duck. She rubbed it, hoping to find some comfort in its feathery touch. It did little good. All her life she had heard people talk about finding comfort in the Bible, finding hope, finding answers, blah, blah, blah. Her mom had become so absorbed in the Bible in the weeks before she died that she hardly found time for anything else, yet look where it had gotten her! She was just as dead. Jenna Rose closed up her bag and left the fuzzy book inside.

Reading a Bible on the school bus? That would nail the coffin on her social standings.

Her body jolted as someone sat down in the seat beside her. No one had ever sat with her before. She looked up to see a dark-skinned guy with a blue Tommy parka zipped all the way up, dark, baggy jeans, and a fitted cap flipped backward over his bald head. He smiled awkwardly as he dropped his heavy backpack on her foot.

"Hi," he stated nervously. His eyes were a gorgeous caramel shade of brown.

Nice come-on. Did you think of that all by yourself?

She smiled briefly in a smug manner, making sure her expression said to him that she was not thrilled about his presence in her seat. He was cute in a thuggish kind of way and all, but with the day she'd had, she didn't need to deal with this creep on her ride home.

The same two guys who had snickered before hooted from the back of the bus.

"I'm Jason," he stated.

Maybe getting her Bible out would scare him away. "Hi," she replied.

Looks like another jock crony to me.

But then again, maybe he wasn't one of those creeps after all.

"I was kinda wondering what you're doing tonight?"

"Plans," she retorted quickly as she began to dig in her bag again.

There has to be something in here to do!

"Okay." He fumbled with his words while also fumbling with his coat's zipper. It was a pretty warm day in late April for having coats zipped up. Jenna Rose hadn't worn a coat in nearly two weeks.

Wonder what he's hiding under there?

His whole thug routine was rather funny in light of his nervousness. Jenna Rose had seen her own share of true thugs while living in Savannah. One thing a real hardcore thug had was a handle on how to win the ladies. This guy was sinking fast. And it was pretty cute. He looked around, then licked his lips in a very LL Cool J imitation and leaned over close to her. "Look, my parents don't get home until six every day. And we've even got a hot tub."

Any trace of intrigue vanished. "Get out of my seat," she stated flatly.

"Wait, if I made a mistake—" he started to say.

"Go."

"You know, I'd like to get to know you a bit first. I'm not thinking you're like *that*," he pleaded. His emphasis on the word aroused the thoughts of the giggling girls moments before.

Great. What's going around this place about me?

"I said get out." This bad dream she called life was quickly turning into a nightmare.

"Come on. What's your name, Mommy?"

" 'Mommy?' Please. Don't make me scream because I will." She turned and stared right into his eyes, begging him to tempt her. She had every intention of doing it too.

"Dude, you're in my seat," someone stated.

Jenna Rose and her seatmate looked up, surprise written on both their faces. Parker stood over Jason's seat with a black ski cap pulled over his hair. Little pieces of curls popped out from under it around his ears and along his neck. He wore a black hoodie with the words "Abortion Is Homicide" and baggy jeans.

Jason the thug looked a bit unsure of himself. "Bro," he pleaded, "can't you see I'm in the middle of a hookup here?"

"Bro," Parker retorted, emphasizing how silly the word sounded coming out of Jason's mouth, "you don't ride this bus, do you?" Jason shook his head.

"If I'm not in my assigned seat, the bus driver freaks, and we'll both end up walking." He clapped a hand down on his adversary's shoulder. "And Bro, it's too far to walk."

Jason jotted his number down on a piece of paper and gave it to Jenna Rose. Rolling her eyes, she accepted it and looked back toward the window. Amy would have crumpled it up and thrown it back at him. He grabbed his bag and got to his feet. Noticing that other kids had witnessed the encounter, he returned to his thuggish facade. Lifting his chin high, he held his arms out and muttered an obscenity close to Parker's face. Parker stood his ground unfazed as the kid took a seat a couple rows behind them.

Jenna Rose surprised herself with a sigh as he sat down in Jason's place. This was the moment her daydreams were made of. She always thought she would be thrilled the day he would finally choose to sit with her, but she didn't find it thrilling at all. Something was going on today. All she wanted was to get home and crawl into her warm little nest of a bed and forget it all happened.

Parker leaned forward, resting his forehead against the seat in front of him so he could see her face better. "You're welcome," he finally stated, flashing that smile that normally melted her.

She rolled her eyes. "Please. Nobody asked you to."

He leaned back. "Yeah, I heard that's your phrase of the day."

Darby McKennitt.

"Word sure travels fast around this place, doesn't it?"

"Yeah, it does when people care about you and want to help you out."

Again she rolled her eyes and found herself fighting back tears. There was no way that Parker Blevins was going to see her cry. Never. A weak laugh escaped her lips. "You care? I've ridden this bus for weeks now and you have never sat with me before, okay? I don't know what you've heard, but you've had your chance and you blew it."

"I haven't heard anything," he replied, digging his hands into the pocket of his hoodie.

"Oh, I'm sure you haven't. Today is the day you chose to come sit with me, and it's just all some big coincidence. Sure. I bet you don't know what's going on."

The bus driver started the bus and barked out orders at the kids in the back.

Eight minutes until I'm home.

"Jenna, what's going on?" Parker asked as the bus started moving. "I heard you were running scared through the school and ditched class. What's that all about?"

"Get out of my seat," she whispered as she closed her eyes and rested her head against the window. All of this was starting to give her a headache. She needed her cookies and her dad.

But he probably was out with his churchies somewhere.

She felt his arm brush against hers and glared at him. "I asked you to move."

He smiled sheepishly. "There are no seats open," he explained. "Unless you want me to go sit on the bus driver's lap. I don't think he'd like that very well. But I would for you."

Oh no. He was not going to make her smile. He was not going to weasel his way into her trust and then smack her with some nasty come-on too.

Who was she kidding? The truth was she had given an invitation to

Parker just days after meeting him. Out of pure desperation to get his attention, she had opened up the door for much more than she had really wanted. He'd had the chance that Jamie or Jason or the creeps who banged on her window thought they should have, yet Parker didn't blow anything. He didn't *take* her invitation. To lump him in with those other guys wasn't really fair to him at all.

She could smell his shampoo faintly as he leaned his head back so he was just barely touching her shoulder. Memories of that day on the corner when she was sure he was going to kiss her raced through her head. That scent had lingered in her thoughts for days afterward. "You don't have to be a lone ranger," he stated, staring at the ceiling of the bus. "You've got people who want to be your friends if you'd just give us a chance."

She so badly wanted to lean her head against his. She didn't want to just be his friend. Instead, she stared out the window again. "Darby said the same thing today," she admitted, her voice barely audible.

"Anyone would be lucky to have Darby McKennitt as a friend. I know I am."

No matter how annoying that girl had been, Jenna Rose believed him. Darby had been nothing but kind to her over and over again from that first smile of acknowledgment in the church parking lot. No one else had given her the slightest bit of attention that day. Maybe she would get lucky enough to find out. . .if she hadn't already blown it for herself.

As they neared her corner, that terrible, lonely feeling she got when she knew they were about to part ways tugged at her gut. She wanted to grab his hand and take him with her and never let him go. But that wasn't possible.

He peered over the seat as they came to a stop. "Will I see you tonight at the shop?"

For the first time all day, Jenna Rose smiled a real smile. "Why, Parker Blevins," she stated in her best Southern accent, "I do believe you are just after me for my voice."

He smiled as he stepped into the aisle to let her out. "I'll see you *and* that voice tonight."

CHAPTER 17

nside, Jenna Rose could hear them going over their set lineup. The *rat-a-tat-tat* of drumsticks on a hard surface and the drone of different voices all speaking at once occasionally sounded. They were probably all there except her. Were they missing her? Technically, she wasn't a member yet. She had still never committed herself to their project. That day they made the circle, she had stayed on the outside, and they had respected her for that.

Unsure of why she was even there, she rested her hand on the door and listened to them talk.

Darby, Parker, Amber, someone come out and invite me in.

By being invited, she was still a guest—she had no responsibility toward them. If she walked in that door on her own, well, then she was making the decision to be accepted by them. And to be part of their band. Was that what she really wanted? Or was she so lonely and craving friendship that she was settling for their company?

She wasn't really sure of the answer. Loneliness was not good company, she knew that much. She had no one. Even Amy was gone—except for a couple of fleeting E-mails about nothing important and about a zillion forwards. There hadn't been a single phone call in weeks. She had talked to Amy's mom and left her message after message, but Amy had never called her back. And everyone here was rejecting her except these people. To walk through that door meant *she* was accepting them.

She listened again as Shanice began to sing. Her voice was

101

strong—not nasally at all like Jenna Rose had first thought. It was soulful and deep. She definitely detected a gospel or rhythm-and-blues influence in the other girl's notes. If Jenna Rose walked away right now and never returned, Shanice would do fine leading this band. Even now—as just a bunch of kids playing in an old storage room—they were better than many of the worship bands she had heard play at the various retreats and church camps she had gone to for most of her life. Second Rate was good. They would do fine without her.

But there really was something unique about this Christian band when the two girls sang together. Add Elijah and his occasional whiteboy suburban hardcore raps in the mix, and they were *really* good. Second Rate was real.

And despite her shortcomings, they wanted her to be a part of it.

Deep down inside of herself, maybe she did too.

She was unsure about what the rumors were going around school. She was pretty certain of their source—Jamie Valentin, but she didn't know exactly what was being said. Had the band members heard Jamie's ugly lies? And what were they going to think when they did? It had to be known in their tight circle that she was after Parker. Even if he wasn't bright enough to pick up on the signs himself, someone in that room had to have seen what was going on by now. So would they think any less of her? Maybe they all thought she was a big flirt or something.

Truthfully, she was still a virgin and had no immediate plans of changing that. She just happened to like guys. She liked being part of a couple. She liked holding hands and kissing and flirting and all that stuff, but she definitely drew a line as to how far it went. She felt a deep emptiness when she wasn't with a guy—something was missing that she just couldn't explain.

She didn't know what was so special about Parker Blevins, but she remained confident that he was the one to fill this void. But whether she would ever see it happen was definitely unknown.

"So is Jenna going to show up?" Andria's voice floated above the sounds of the two pizza makers in the background.

Jenna Rose strained to hear what was said. "She'll be here," Parker replied confidently.

"I don't know," added Darby. "I think I really upset her. I didn't mean to. . . ."

Jenna Rose smiled, guilt telling her to make up her mind quickly as to what she was doing.

"She'll be here," Parker stated again.

His confidence was reassuring. It felt good and right. For some reason, most of the things he said felt that way.

It's the point of no return. Here goes nothing. . . .

She pushed the door open.

Parker sprung to his feet as she entered, excitedly attacking Darby with a finger flick to her ear. She squealed, attempting to fend him off with fleeting open-hand blows, but he was undeterred. "I told you she would be here," he sang. Jenna Rose grinned and remembered the pathetic cabbage patch dance he did the last time she saw him this excited. He held himself in check from dancing and settled back into his chair.

Elijah pulled another chair up and patted it for Jenna Rose to take a seat with them. "Welcome to the round table," he stated. "Just ignore the fact that it's square. Details are so unimportant."

She smiled and sat down.

No one told me to leave or anything!

The whole group was hovering over a pile of wadded-up notebook papers as well as several still-smooth ones. Jenna Rose stole a glance to see that they were song titles scribbled in different orders. They were trying to come up with a set order. "Awesome God," and "Did You Feel the Mountains Tremble?" All songs she knew well.

Parker leaned over and stretched an arm around Jenna Rose's shoulder.

For someone who doesn't seem to get a clue, he sure is touchy-feely.

Not that she was complaining. This happened to be her favorite part of band practice. They turned and looked at one another, their noses only inches apart. Fighting back the desire to lean over just a bit more and kiss him, Jenna Rose wrinkled up her nose in a playful way at him. He smiled in return.

He is just so cute.

"Okay, everyone." He broke the silence. "We've got an announcement to make."

Elijah thumped a beat on the table. Andria quickly had to show him up with a more complicated finger drumroll. Catching her hand, Elijah entwined his fingers in hers. If those two really were dating, Jenna Rose suddenly realized she had never seen any sign of it other than some handholding and when Elijah had rested his head in her lap a few days earlier. They definitely made a good couple. Jenna Rose had to shake her head however at the sight of their matching black fingernail polish. She could totally see Andria painting his nails as they listened to one of those freaky Christian bands. Andria caught her eye and smiled warmly. Looking into Elijah's face, she then gave his hand a tight squeeze.

Two weird peas in a pod.

"Wednesday," Parker continued, "we have a photo shoot."

Darby giggled. "That sounds so serious. It's just my cousin Chance."

Parker rolled his eyes playfully and smacked her lightly on the back of the head. Turning to Andria he asked, "What in the world did you feed her today? She is wired."

Andria just shrugged and rested her chin on the tabletop. "Who knows with her and the weird stuff she eats? And by the way, Chance is a photography major at KSU," she reminded her sister. "Chance's cool."

"I know he is," Darby replied as she balled back up into her usual defensive self. "I'm related to him too."

"He's going to shoot three rolls, so that's like seventy pics, right?" Parker continued, elbowing Darby occasionally as he spoke. "So, we're going to have a ton to work with."

"What are we going to do with seventy pics?" Shanice asked, fumbling with the stack of papers.

Elijah jumped in. "Tons of stuff. Flyers. Promo stuff. Our CD cover and insert."

"Hey!" Andria shot up. "T-shirts! We could make T-shirts!"

"They probably won't all turn out," Amber added. Jenna Rose nodded in agreement. That girl was so quiet that most of the time she forgot Amber was there. "Honestly, there will be less than that to chose from," Amber continued.

"What are we wearing?" Darby asked. "I don't care as long as it's not cheesy Brady Bunch matching costumes."

Elijah sat up quickly, a giant smile crossing his face. Before he could speak, Andria had a hand over his mouth. "Don't even think about it."

Shanice and Andria shot one another excited glances, each dancing in their seat. "Shopping!" they yelled together.

Parker nodded, tightening his squeeze on Jenna Rose. "I think it's about time we take Jenna here shopping. Shopping Second Rate style." He gave her his best grin.

"Oh no." Jenna Rose tried to wiggle out of his embrace. "I don't think I like the sound of that."

But it could be fun, couldn't it?

Darby snatched up her arm, attempting to yank her to her feet. Still locked in her seat by Parker, Jenna Rose screamed in laughter as she tried to deter Darby's efforts. It felt good to laugh, to *really* laugh again. It had been way too long.

Finally, with the help of some side tickling from Parker, she resigned herself to their mercy and allowed them to drag her from the room. They piled into the Angelinos' SUV, laughing and singing. Mrs. Angelino grinned warmly at each band member but saved her widest smile for Jenna Rose. She looked like she was about to burst with pride at the sight of her. "It's good to see you, sweetie. That voice of yours is straight from heaven."

Jenna Rose returned the smile and nodded as she climbed in.

As Mrs. Angelino pulled out of the parking lot, Andria leaned forward and massaged Jenna Rose's shoulders like a boxing trainer. "I have been looking forward to the day I got to dress you myself," she stated slyly. "We need the camera now. This is going to be fun."

"No, no, no," Jenna Rose replied through her laughter. "I'll dress myself, thank you."

"Ah, but you have to fit into the band. We have an image to maintain."

"Yeah," Elijah added, turning up the Southern gospel tape in his aunt's radio, "we can't have anyone on stage looking like they belong at a Gaithers' concert."

"A Gaithers' concert? I do not dress like I belong in a Gaithers' concert," Jenna Rose protested.

Parker gave Jenna Rose a quick once-over. "I think they're being a little harsh," he agreed approvingly.

Jenna Rose slumped back in her seat, trying to pretend like she was pouting. This time she wasn't doing a very good job. Her adrenaline was pumping just having Parker sitting next to her, his arm against hers. That alone made this whole decision worth it.

I'm going shopping at a thrift store. What would Savannah think of me now? Well, new friends or not, they can forget about anti-abortion and Jesus freak shirts. She wouldn't be caught dead in either of those. And those Converse skater shoes? *Not in a million years!*

"What are we doing for the photo shoot then?" Darby asked.

"Chance and I have it all worked out," Parker stated. "We're taking a road trip and we'll see where it takes us. We want quirky pictures."

"You? Quirky?" Jenna Rose teased. She was feeling very empowered by her new sense of belonging. "Never!" she found herself stating the word with Darby. They turned and looked at each other and laughed. That was probably a good sign.

Her body tightened at the sight of the Salvation Army Thrift Store sign as Mrs. Angelino drove the SUV into the parking lot.

Time to take the plunge into total freakdom—she was shopping at a thrift store, and on purpose even. If Jamie or Denise or any of those people saw her go into this store, it would all be over. If Amy only knew what Ohio had done to her!

CHAPTER 18

Wow." The word actually escaped her mouth before she could contain it. Parker swatted at her with his elbow, obviously giddy with excitement at her reaction. The room before them was large and, except for a slightly dusty smell drifting through the cleaning agents, very tidy. The various sections of the store were marked with big, colorful signs, and the clothes hung on circular showcases.

Jenna Rose had never been in a thrift store other than doing volunteer work at the free stores in the inner-city missions in Savannah and Atlanta. Those places were always understaffed and highly disorganized, with handmade signs scrawled on the back of cardboard or old computer paper. She had wondered how anyone could ever find anything in them. Often times, she had dug through piles of unfolded, mix-matched clothes for harried mothers with screaming little children running between the table legs and kicking her in the shins. Oh yeah, she loved kids.

Thrift stores were the one place she never thought she would purposely find herself in.

And here she was about to go shopping. For herself, nonetheless. Amy would be beside herself in laughter right now.

As she let Darby drag her by the hand to a display of shirts, she made a mental checklist of things they would not, under any circumstances, talk her into. Ties over T-shirts, suspenders, skater shoes—*used shoes at all—ew*—and hats. *Not going to do any of them.* Shanice grabbed a rickety-wheeled cart and followed.

Jenna Rose dug into her pocket and pulled out the few dollar bills that were wadded up haphazardly. "I only have four bucks," she stated, hoping it would get her out in the clear.

"That's plenty to get you an outfit," Shanice replied as she flipped through a rack of T-shirts. "Oh, an old Transformers shirt!" She held up the red T-shirt for the rest to see. Most of its screened picture of a yellow Transformer robot had flaked away around the edges, but the picture was still intact. "One of us will fit into this." She dropped it into the cart.

"Oh, I like this," Jenna Rose blurted out, tossing a pale yellow Abercrombie tee in the cart.

Andria quickly fished it out. "No way. Not in a million years." She put it back on the rack and smiled at Jenna Rose. "I'm in charge, remember?"

Elijah climbed onto the front of the cart. "I wonder if I would fit," he mused, eyeing the child seat.

Shanice yanked the cart out from under him. He stumbled backwards, almost landing on his backside. "I don't think so!" Shanice ordered. "I don't feel like getting kicked out this time. I want to finish my shopping."

Jenna Rose smiled and went back to her rack. She was shopping with people who got kicked out of thrift stores. She was here by her own free will. Yesterday, she would have laughed at someone had such a thing been suggested. She hadn't even known people *could* get kicked out of thrift stores. "Four dollars is going to buy me an outfit?" she blurted out as what Shanice had said to her registered. "Are you serious?"

Shanice nodded, throwing a whimsical flowery shirt with winglike arms at her. "Here you go. You can be the hippy. 'All we are saying is give peace a chance. . . ,' " she sang, dramatically swaying back and forth.

"Maybe if it were a costume party we were shopping for." Jenna Rose hung the shirt back up and continued to dig. Amber yanked it back off the rack and returned it to the cart behind her. Turning back to Darby, Jenna Rose spotted Andria returning with her arms loaded down. The drummer smiled at her, a wicked, rotten, but friendly smile.

Darby returned to the group empty-handed. "Nothing here," she stated, flipping through the stack of clothes her sister had plopped into the cart. "Andi, what is some of this stuff?"

That was enough to convince Jenna Rose. "Huh-uh," she exclaimed, diving into the stack of clothes. "I'm not putting on anything any of the rest of you wouldn't wear."

"There's your first mistake," Parker stated, throwing in a pair of camouflage pants, "because Elijah will wear anything."

" 'Tis true, 'tis true," his friend replied, a red straw golf hat with a flowered band and monogrammed shark perched on his head. "Except maybe this thing." He tossed it smoothly back into the hat bin.

"Okay. I'm not putting on anything any of you other girls won't wear," Jenna Rose corrected herself.

"I'd wear anything in here," Andria retorted swiftly. "Just to prove it to you, you can pick out my outfit. Whatever you choose, that's what I'll wear tomorrow."

"How about the Abercrombie shirt?" Jenna Rose shot off at her, grabbing it off the rack.

"Except that," she replied stubbornly.

Parker threw Andria a cowboy hat with a brim that curved up dramatically on the sides. Elijah intercepted it in midair. "Now this one is cool!" he exclaimed, placing it slowly on his head. He snorted and pulled at his baggy green work pants. He examined the well-worn straw cowboy hat and then tossed it into the cart. "If I'm going to wear the hat, then I need a belt!" He took off again toward the men's department.

"He's like a kid in a candy store in here, isn't he?" Jenna Rose remarked to Parker as they walked along side by side. With a quick flick of the wrist, she could easily grab his hand, but she hesitated. Things were going well, and she didn't want to ruin them. Every now and then, she made sure her hand lightly brushed against his, hoping that he would take her hand in his.

"He's just plain odd, that's all he is," Parker replied.

Did he just tap my hand back? Or was it my imagination?

Whatever the case, he still hadn't taken hold of her hand like she had hoped.

Andria rolled her eyes and continued pushing the cart down the rows. "He can be such a dork." Jenna Rose was a bit captivated by the swishing sound Andria's lightweight baggy pants made as she walked. They flared over her shoes and drug slightly on the ground in the back. Tiny belts connected the various pockets and wrapped around the inside of her legs.

I bet she never walks into the mall except to go to that freaky Goth store.

Jenna Rose had once found herself drawn in at the sight of a Care Bear tee, but she found herself scarred for life by the time she left. If Andria had never been in there, she should go.

As they piled the clothes on the checkout counter, Andria collected money from everyone. Jenna Rose debated for a moment on whether or not to give Andria all of her four dollars. Chances were slim that she would honestly ever wear any of these clothes after Wednesday. She wasn't even sure she wanted to wear them *Wednesday.* Then again, the others were all just pitching in money and buying it all at once, as a group. *Oh, I might as well,* Jenna sighed to herself and reluctantly handed over all of her cash.

They thanked the cashier and headed back out to their waiting driver. Mrs. Angelino sat in the SUV beating on her steering wheel in laughter as Mark Lowry ranted about kids and vacations on the current tape. Climbing into the middle seat, Darby asked Jenna Rose if she thought her dad would let her spend the night at their house.

"I don't know," she replied, rather amazed at the fact that she honestly was hoping he would let her. "What with it being a school night and all."

"We have a few hours," Andria added. "It's not even six yet."

Jenna Rose dug for her cell phone to call her dad and let him know she was going to the twins' house.

That should make his day.

She was startled when he answered after one ring. "Hi, Dad," she stated.

"Where have you been? You didn't leave me a note." He sounded a bit perturbed.

Yeah, you never leave me a note.

"I'm with the twins," she replied, smiling at Darby.

How weird is this?

"And some other kids from church."

"You are? The McKennitt twins?"

"Do you want to talk to one of them?" she sighed. Why should he honestly believe her? She had been going out of her way for weeks now to avoid them.

"No, no," he argued, quickly changing his tone. "That's great. Wow, you're really with the twins?"

"Dad!"

"Well, what do you need?"

"Is it all right if I go over to their house for a bit?"

"To their house? Seriously?"

She couldn't keep herself from laughing anymore. He sounded like he wanted to come through the phone and jump for joy. She could picture him sitting flabbergasted behind his desk in the dining-room office. Soon he'd be throwing his hands up, praising God, and then laughing to himself. He always did that when he was sure he'd just received an answer to prayer.

"Yes, Dad. . .to their house. Is it okay?"

"Well, it is a school night," he stated.

There he goes trying to sound all fatherly just to save face.

"Just call me when you're ready to come home, and I'll pick you up," he conceded.

She agreed and hung up the phone.

I am on my way to hang out at the Olsen-Manson twins' house. How weird is that?

She folded her phone back over and tucked it away in her messenger bag. Parker had his arm around the seat as he chatted with Elijah about the song orders. She wanted to reach up over her shoulder and pull his hand down on her instead of the seat, but she fumbled with her bag instead. He smiled at her and focused back on Elijah.

Well, here goes nothing. I'm going to hang out at the Freak Sisters' house. If only Amy could see her now. . .she'd disown her.

CHAPTER 19

The five girls waved as the large vehicle backed out of the driveway. Mrs. Angelino sounded off two long blasts of the horn and waved back. Before turning the corner, Parker stuck his head out the window and yelled, "We'll be over after dinner!"

Darby swung her arms excitedly in reply as they disappeared around the corner.

I could walk here.

The McKennitt twins lived about five blocks away from Jenna Rose, in the opposite direction from where Parker lived. It was another one of those developments where everything didn't look exactly the same. The Brinley family would never be able to live in a neighborhood like this on her dad's salary. Maybe when she became rich and famous.

Jenna Rose surveyed the house in front of her. A curved stone walkway led through beds of colorful spring flowers to a two-story brick colonial house. Trimmed neatly with cream-colored shutters, the house was surrounded by large white-barked birch trees and English ivy. She followed her hosts up the paved driveway to the back door.

Even the backyard was perfect. White picket fencing surrounded a vegetable garden plot near the back of the property. A cute little garden shed complete with front porch and window boxes in matching cream sat nearby. Tucked away in the corner next to the wooden deck that jutted off the back of the house was a small koi pond surrounded by flowers. Birds fluttered from the many bird feeders and houses spread through the trees. To Jenna Rose, sitting out here just listening to their music would be a perfect enough way to spend time. Two adirondack chairs made a cozy resting spot under another one of the birch trees. A red maple with its crimson leaves shaded a children's playhouse and molded plastic sandbox.

What is up with this obsession I have with flowers lately?

Darby hurried her along as they took their bag of thrift store finds and mounted the back stairs off the kitchen to the second floor. Dawdling, Jenna Rose tried to soak in as much of the house as she could. This place was heaven, and she wanted to see every inch of it. Like that other staircase. In the movies, only houses with a grand front staircase ever had a back staircase leading to the kitchen. She wanted to see it all.

At the end of the hall, Andria opened a door and the others followed. A gasp escaped Jenna Rose as she entered.

Shanice nodded. "Pretty cool, isn't it? Their mom is an interior decorator."

"And one of the coolest people you will ever know," Amber added.

For a fleeting moment, Jenna Rose wondered what they would have thought of her mother. Before she got sick, man, she was cool. If she had beaten the illness and been there like most moms are, her daughter would have probably been more like them—seemingly confident in her beliefs and proud of her faith. Maybe not a walking Jesus billboard but at least someone who knew what she stood for. Jenna Rose had been well on her way until her world fell apart around her. Now she just did the best to pretend for her dad's sake. It used to be a lot easier to accept when things were good.

She still couldn't believe her eyes. The room was just amazing. A fluffy orange shag rug covered the green hardwood floor. Two sitting areas built into the walls formed an L-shaped sofa covered in pillows of various sizes, shapes, and colors. On the floor were two giant neon green beanbag chairs that sat opposite the sofa. Closest to the door, the walls were built with floor-to-ceiling shelving that held books, games, CDs, and numerous little knick-knacks and stuffed animals. In one corner a steel desk fashioned from scrap metal and pipes housed a green computer. A small television and stereo sat on a stand in the other corner. A door in the far wall appeared to lead to a bathroom.

"It's like a set off of MTV or something," Jenna Rose mused as she ran her fingers over the tie-dyed paint job on the wall—the same orange as the rug was mixed with yellow, green, blue, and a small touch of red. A couple of Christian rock band posters hung in frames on the wall.

"Our mom did some design work for a Much Music set last year," Darby replied, "but never MTV."

Well, who would have known two Goth chicks would be interested in Austin Powers' décor?

Purple and black with gargoyles and candles would have been more likely. This was definitely not what she had expected out of them.

Jenna Rose followed Amber to the sofa and sat down. Uncertainty still surrounded her decision about being there. At least there weren't any Ouija boards on their stack of games. If anyone said a word about piercing anything, she wasn't even calling her dad—she was out of there. She'd walk.

Shanice cranked up the stereo and started to dance to the ska music that blasted forth.

Why are Christian kids the only people in the world who actually listen to ska?

But it was pretty fun music.

"Where did the disco ball go?" Shanice asked as she flipped the light switch.

"It was trashed. Cheap thing never did really work that well," Darby stated as she dumped the bag of clothes out on the rug. "Mom's looking for a retro one. We should figure out what we're wearing before the guys get here."

"Why didn't they come in with us?" Jenna Rose asked. Being with them minus Parker was just weird.

"Guys aren't allowed in the house until one of the parental units are home," Andria replied as she flopped down on the rug alongside the clothes.

114

They actually follow that rule?

Jenna Rose wasn't sure that she'd ever had a friend who did. You just made sure the guy knew when to head out the front door when dear old Dad was heading in the back.

Just another oddity about this group.

Darby disappeared through the bathroom door and returned with an oak-framed floor mirror.

Maybe they should adopt me.

Ever since she was a little girl, Jenna Rose had wanted a mirror like that—a beautiful mirror she could see her princess dresses in, her prom dress, her wedding gown. But she had never gotten it. . .and probably never would. Too expensive or some equally lame excuse. The closest she ever got was a cheap full-length mirror mounted on the back of her closet door. Her princess dress-up clothes' true sparkle was diminished in its flimsy reflection.

"We used to have different rooms," Darby said to Jenna Rose as she placed the mirror near them, "but we always ended up in each other's rooms at night to talk and stuff. For our twelfth birthday, we got our own recreation room here and now we share a bedroom."

"Yeah, they're totally spoiled," Shanice stated, grinning as she started to rummage through the pile. She found the Transformer shirt and pulled it over the blue baby tee she was wearing. It hugged her form and ended just a bit longer than her belt loops.

If Shanice can't wear that, none of the rest of us could. There's no way I could get that over my body.

It escaped her why they had bought a little boy's shirt.

"Yeah, right," Andria complained. "I still demand my own computer, and until that day, I can't be called spoiled."

Darby rolled her eyes. "She thinks I spend too much time on the computer, but all she wants it for is to chat. The only person I really ever talk to online is Amber when we send music files back and forth." Amber smiled sheepishly at Jenna Rose. "I write the words and piddle with the music, but Amber is the one who makes it a real song."

115

"Nice, Shanice, that looks great."

Wow. Amber did more than push buttons and follow Parker's lead? Jenna Rose couldn't quite picture her as anything more than their tag-along. "Why isn't the band performing your songs, Darby?" Jenna Rose asked. If her music was as good as Parker kept raving about, it didn't make sense that they were performing the same old worship songs hundreds of other bands were doing. There were only so many ways to sing "El Shaddai."

"We will be," Andria jumped in, looking a bit upset that Jenna Rose was questioning her sister, "when Miss Perfection decides that she has them just right."

"Well, if this is the material we're going to use as our own, then I do want it just right," Darby defended. "Parker and I think it's almost ready."

Parker and I.

Those words coming out of the mouth of someone aside from herself struck a nerve. Jenna Rose didn't like the sound of that at all. Then again, it made sense. If there was a "Parker and I" here already, Darby would be the perfect candidate for it. They talked about each other all the time. What had Parker said just hours ago on the bus?

Anyone would be lucky to have Darby McKennitt as a friend. I know I am.

If they were as discreet about their relationship as her sister and Elijah were, that would explain why she hadn't picked up on any signs.

This is just my luck.

Andria pulled on the camouflage pants Parker had picked out. They hung loosely around her waist—the only thing keeping them up being the slight curve to her hips. "Parker can forget about getting these."

My goodness, girl, you look like a dork. I can't believe I'm actually here doing this! "They're too long," Jenna Rose pointed out. Andria's feet had disappeared into the cuffs. The redhead bounded to the desk, fished out a pair of scissors and slipped the pants off.

"Not anymore," she replied as she measured quickly and hacked off part of the legs in three quick snips. Tossing the scissors into the pile, she wiggled back into the pants.

"Now they're too short," Darby and Jenna Rose chorused. Andria tossed a nearby pillow at them and looked down at her pants. She had cut them off about two inches above her ankles.

"Do I hem them or not?" she asked, turning her attention to the other girls.

"No way," Shanice replied.

"They're too short," stated Jenna Rose again.

"Nah." Shanice shook her head. "They're perfect."

Add another item to my never-gonna-happen list.

"Don't expect me to wear something like that. I draw the line there," Jenna Rose hinted.

A silly, wicked little cackle coming from Andria cut her off. "You draw the line nowhere, newbie. You just wait and see what you're wearing."

CHAPTER 220

I can't believe that's me. Jenna Rose stared at her reflection in the cheap full-length mirror tacked on the back of her closet door. A day after the thrift-store shopping spree and despite knowing what was coming, she was clad in clothes that she never thought would ever cross her body.

Darby, dressed in a pair of gray hip huggers and a black half-sleeve tee with the words "blah, blah, blah" emblazoned in small white letters across the chest, stood just behind her, positively glowing. Taking Jenna Rose by the shoulders, she danced a jig and giggled dramatically. "You look so good."

No, I don't. I'm the one who looks like a dork. What a hoax this is!

Andria had done her sister's hair by taking the top half of it and pulling it into two toddlerlike ponytails on the sides of her head. Jenna Rose was just glad that Andria didn't decide to do that to her instead.

"Do I really have to do the pants?" she queried, looking down at her legs. Jenna Rose had been one of the first to jump on the capri pants' bandwagon, but black low-waist capris with white stitching and bell-flared bottoms were just way too far out there for her. "I have a pair of flared jeans or two that might look good."

You get up on stage and everyone is going to see right through this image. Fake.

Elijah's voice boomed up the stairs. "We need to go in like five minutes ago, girls! Chance is going to be waiting for us."

118

Bouncing as she sat on Jenna Rose's peach floral comforter, Andria shook her head to the previous clothing request. "You agreed."

Amber, once again dressed more conservatively than the rest in a pair of jeans and a festival T-shirt dating from a few years ago, nodded sympathetically in unison.

Why doesn't anyone pick on her for her clothing choices?

She had agreed, however. Again, she surveyed the pants, turning around to look at the rearview as well. Maybe with different shoes. . .

Secretly, she loved the shirt. The beat-up Transformer print was not her first choice, but she loved the way the shirt fit. It was soft, well-worn cotton that felt good on her arms even though it looked tight. In no way had she ever thought she was endowed in the chest area, but after seeing that shirt on twiggy little Shanice, she had never guessed it would stretch to fit her. It did and it looked good. With her arms in the air, she spun again to see how far up it rode. The low-waist capris made her nervous— she didn't need a plumber-thing going on while singing "Awesome God" in front of a church revival audience. The shirt barely touched the waist of the capris and didn't allow any of her skin to show. Not her usual choice in clothing style, but it would do for the band. Personally, she saw nothing wrong with showing just a little skin.

Kicking a foot out to look at the black low-cut boot with oversized tread and red-striped gym socks, Jenna Rose desperately sought an excuse to ditch the footwear. Gym socks sporting colored stripes that were made to be pulled up over the calves should be outlawed by the fashion police. They were hideous. The pants she could deal with. And she could sleep and lounge in that shirt all the time, but the boots and socks had to go. Especially with capris.

"Don't even think about the boots," Andria stated as she slipped her feet back into her light blue Sauconys. "You're wearing them too."

Jenna Rose clasped her gold cross necklace around her neck. If she were going to be part of a Christian band, the cross would probably be a good choice. Darby had given her a handful of black flimsy bracelets. She fumbled with them, trying to decide what was the best way to wear them. As they could hear the guys downstairs getting antsy again, Andria took two from her and crossed them together in two C shapes to form one big bracelet. Jenna Rose let her put it on her right arm while she let the others fall loose on her left.

I think I once got bracelets like this out of a quarter machine when I was five and thought I was the coolest.

"I still hate the socks," Jenna Rose mumbled as she turned herself away from the mirror for their inspection. She threw her arms in the air dramatically and spun slowly around. "They don't match."

"Exactly!" Shanice retorted. Her orange zip-away pants had not been part of the thrift store loot, but the blue high school softball shirt with the numbers "03" on the back had been one of the first things tossed in the cart. The vintage shirt was layered over another form-fitting white tee that peeked out at the neck and the hem. Her hair was braided into precise lines tight against her head, which led back into long, thin, copper-beaded braids.

It must have taken someone forever to do that.

"That's the purpose of wearing the socks unmatched, Jenna Rose," Shanice explained. "Whose rule is it that your socks have to match? Who cares?" Darby gave her a high-five in agreement.

Oh well. I mean, it's just for some pictures. Who will really see them anyway?

She took one last look in the mirror. Thankfully, her hair remained relatively tame—they just parted it down the middle and added a very generous amount of curl gel to define her natural curls. It looked a bit messy for her taste as some strands curled into much tighter spirals than others, but it didn't look bad.

Maybe I should have worn this to school today. If anything I did could have scared off Jamie Valentin, this would be it.

Hopefully, Jamie Valentin and his crew would find a new flavor-of-the-month soon and just leave her alone.

"What happened with the dance tryouts, Jenna?" Shanice asked as she scrunched the blond's hair once more before their exit. "You haven't said anything about it all week."

Jenna Rose shrugged her shoulders and pretended that it really didn't matter to her. "I couldn't really tell you what happened, but I suppose I should take no news as not-so-good news. I haven't heard anything."

"Sorry to hear that," Darby said as she tossed makeup haphazardly into a small carrying bag. "I know it meant a lot to you."

Again Jenna Rose shrugged. There was no real use going into why it meant a lot to her. She probably didn't even know why herself. "Not a big deal."

"We didn't need them cutting into our rehearsal time anyway," Shanice declared, flashing Jenna Rose her first smile.

She returned the smile warmly.

That's right. I'm the lead singer of a band now.

Jenna Rose followed Andria as they bounded down the stairs. Finally, after mustering up the courage partway down the steps, she reached out and brushed her hand over the other girl's spikes. They were just as bristly hard as they looked. Andria turned around. "You had a fuzzy," Jenna Rose lied. She didn't want to look like an idiot and say, "I just wanted to touch your hair."

Now when I finally get the courage to touch Parker's curls, there won't be any apologizing.

Soon. Very, very soon.

And hopefully over a kiss.

Andria was clad in her cutoff camouflage pants and a red spaghetti-strap tee with a small cross made from sequins hanging at her chest. On her feet she wore a pair of cheap blue flip-flops. Her jewelry was much heavier than that of the other girls—earrings, toe rings, bracelets, rings, and a black choker with a silver fish medallion. Her bangs were parted in the middle and brushed flat in either direction while the rest of her hair had been painstakingly spiked in every direction. Even the tiniest little hairs on the back of her neck were spiked straight out.

Parker and Elijah were perched on the front porch, talking idly with a college guy Jenna Rose could only assume was Chance. His windblown hair was the same mousy brown color as Darby's and hung in his eyes and well past his ears.

With a squeal, Andria rushed into his arms. They hugged, rocking back and forth wildly. "I haven't seen you in forever!" she exclaimed. "Thank you so much for doing this."

The guest pulled his other cousin in close for a hug as well and smiled at the others. "We ready to get this on?"

Jenna Rose jumped with a start at the sound of her own voice cheering with the others. That tingle returned as Parker grabbed her hand and they ran toward the old Chevy minivan that Chance drove. She was actually excited. Their first photo shoot!

The first of many.

Parker's optimism was starting to rub off on her. Helping her into the bench seat in the back, Parker squeezed in close beside her. Amber followed and sat on the other side of him. The twins and Shanice piled into the middle bench while Elijah took the passenger seat.

Chance climbed in and started the engine. "Before we get started, I think we should grab some grub and chat. That way I can get a feel for what it is you guys are all about and try to get that in the pics."

"Our instruments are at the shop," Parker called up as he wrapped his arms around both girls, squeezing them across the shoulders. Jealousy swept over Jenna Rose.

At least it's just Amber and not Darby.

As heartless as she felt thinking it, she did find some comfort in the other girl's plain-Jane persona—especially if she was as musically gifted as they all made her out to be. She definitely wasn't one for many words.

"In the mood for pizza?" Elijah asked. "I got connections."

"I think we should do a few shots with our instruments anyway," Darby added. Surprisingly, she didn't have her guitar with her now.

Chance agreed and headed toward the shop.

One patron looked up uneasily as the group entered the restaurant. Jenna Rose's heart skipped as she watched the woman put her foot on her purse and scoot closer to her toddler as they walked past.

And they like people reacting to them this way?

For a midweek afternoon, the dining room was unexpectedly full.

Let's just get to the back room.

All these adult eyes on her looking like some skater chick or something was unnerving. What they must be thinking of the preacher's daughter now!

Elijah hurried to the kitchen while Andria and Amber started grabbing and refilling patrons' drinks. Parker and Shanice quickly cleaned an empty table.

I thought we came here to eat, not work.

Jenna Rose suddenly felt very much like the new kid on the block. Did they expect her to jump in and do something too? And if so, what was it? Obviously, this was something they had done before. Taking a broom, Darby glanced over her shoulder at her cousin and Jenna Rose. "Why don't you guys go head into the back? We'll be there in a minute."

"Anything I can do to help?" Chance asked, pushing in the chairs at the now spotless table as Parker carried the busboy tub back to the kitchen.

Of course he had to ask and make me look selfish.

Jenna Rose shuffled her feet nervously.

"That's all right," Darby replied. "We like to help out when it looks like they need it. We owe them with letting us use the room and all the pop and pizza we go through. We'll just be a minute."

Mrs. Angelino emerged from the kitchen waving her hands in the air as she pushed the teens through the door. "Out, out, out," she bellowed in her tough but kind voice. "I will have none of that. Thank you for your help, but the day that Papa and I can't take care of the restaurant on our own will be the day that we close it down. So go do your thing." Elijah scooped up the busboy tub and carried it back to the sink. "Nipote, you too. Go."

"Won't take but a minute to do these dishes," he argued.

"A minute? What? And I'll be doing them over again because they aren't clean. No thank you. Go, nipote, and be with your band."

Elijah looked at her stubbornly and held his ground. She reached out and snatched the scrub pad from his hand. Real love showed in his eyes as he hugged her and hurried past. Jenna Rose watched with guilty interest and wondered what was so terrible about his parents that he had to live with his aunt and uncle instead. Parker had said Elijah's family was "a mess," so that had to mean that they were still around enough for him to know. At least he seemed to be in a good situation now.

The afternoon went by in a whirlwind as they joked and talked while munching on pizza and breadsticks. Chance talked at intervals, occasionally asking questions and discussing dorm life. His camera flashed periodically as they ate.

"Can you do a short rehearsal?" Chance asked. "I don't want staged photos. I want shots of you guys doing what you do best, how you do it."

As they entered the rehearsal room, Jenna Rose wanted to pull the blinds. The sun filtering through the holes like that first day would just be the perfect setting. She found herself hesitant, waiting for someone else to suggest it. She was the new girl. Was it really her place to make suggestions like that already? The memory of Elijah and his cross tee with the light shining on it just right flashed through her mind. That was perfect for what they were trying to do here. They would probably never be able to stage it that way again.

Everyone took his or her place as Chance fumbled with a lens in the corner.

"What are we playing, Jenna?" Parker asked as he strummed a chord.

Jenna Rose tried to hide her surprise. They were asking her? She chose a song and counted off to start.

Chance's camera flashed constantly as they played.

Jenna Rose beamed the entire time, giddy with excitement over the show in a few days and the reality of it all. People were going to see her sing not because they had to, but because they wanted to. And best of all, Parker was going to be right there with her. Maybe, just maybe, they were going to get over that hump. . . .

As the late spring sun began to descend, Chance announced that he wanted to go on a road trip. "You guys all have some money? I know a place pretty fun where we can get some pics that I think will really reflect who you are."

"Sounds great," Shanice replied as they followed him out to the van.

"After you," Jenna Rose stated as she let Amber in ahead of her. Parker was going to be all hers this time. It was too bad they couldn't have a seat completely to themselves. She followed the quiet girl in, leaving Parker to be the closest person to the door.

"We ready?" Chance called as the engine fired up.

"Let's do it!" Parker yelled, banging the door shut. He threw an arm up around Jenna Rose.

Here goes nothing. . . .

All in the same motion, Jenna Rose met his hand as he placed it on her shoulder. Interlocking their fingers, she caressed the palm of his hand with her thumb and pulled his arm down across her back instead of the seat. She didn't dare turn around and look at his face for fear of rejection.

He's probably clueless.

Biting her bottom lip to fight back a smile, she wanted to yell out in joy as he reworked his fingers through hers and let the back of his hand relax against her arm.

"I'm going to let you take one or two rolls today to get developed on your own," Chance added. "If I were you, I would make a flyer with a photo and then do some distributing at school before your show Saturday. That way people will start associating your faces with the music."

"We can do that," Elijah replied.

Staring at the back of Darby's head for what seemed like an eternity, she felt the pins and needles start to creep into the arm that was crossed awkwardly across her body to hold Parker's hand. There was no way she was letting go. As the feeling got stronger and stronger, she squirmed, trying to decide what she could do without letting go of his grip. Finally, she turned away from him, leaning her body back against his side. The strange sensation in her arm subsided almost immediately. She snuggled her head down into his shoulder, gleeful that the feeling of his closeness was all that she had imagined it would be.

Still uneasy about witnessing his reaction, she just let her eyes fall shut. The feel of his hand on hers was enough answer for now.

Wherever this road trip takes us, I hope we take forever to get there.

If only all these other people weren't here. She wanted to turn around and talk to him, try to put into words how she felt. She didn't really know how she felt, but that didn't matter. She finally had the guts to let him know there was something there like she had never felt with anyone before him. There was no way this conversation could happen in front of other people—their friends or otherwise.

Our friends? That feels weird to say.

As she opened her eyes, she spied Amber looking at her intently.

Are you jealous?

The quiet girl turned her head quickly and looked out the window. Jenna Rose bit her lip again. For a brief moment, she had detected something in Amber's gaze before the girl looked away. Was it jealousy? Or was it something else?

CHAPTER 21

The lunchroom before her was much less daunting with Darby's bright smile beckoning her to a table under the five-a-day poster. For a brief moment she entertained the thought of joining Denise, Lora, and the senior dance team leader at their table by the window. Just a simple hi-and-did-that-creep-Jamie-Valentin-really-keep-me-from-receiving-a-spot-on-the-dance-team kind of thing. Somehow, the magnitude of not making the team had diminished since Monday. She really didn't care. She couldn't pinpoint why it wasn't as important anymore, but it just wasn't. The past few days seemed like ages ago.

She joined Darby, scanning the lunchroom once again for any sign of Jamie Valentin.

"You okay?" Darby asked as she arranged her silverware around her tan plastic tray.

"Yeah," came the reply. She had followed Darby's advice and started taking her own lunch. It figured that today Darby would have a tray in front of her.

Got to know what days to pack and what days to eat here. Note to self: Pizza must be a winner around here.

She seemed to be the only one in the whole lunchroom with a packed lunch. "Just watching for someone," Jenna Rose added.

Darby inquired, "Oh yeah? Who?" She chomped into the pizza, cheese stringing from her mouth.

127

"Nobody important." Jenna Rose bit into her turkey-on-wheat, rather glad that she had brought her own lunch. Honestly, she was getting a bit tired of pizza with all that they ate at rehearsals. There were only so many ways to fix pizza in one week. The Angelinos made good pizza, but one could only take so much before feeling a little pepperoni-y.

"The same nobody you were running from a couple days ago?" Darby prodded gently, trying to catch her eye.

Jenna Rose dropped her head instantly. "No," she replied. There was *some* honesty in the word—she had been running from Mullet Boy that day, and now she was looking for Jamie. She wasn't completely dishonest.

"Well, I really wish you would tell me what that was all about," stated Darby as she returned her focus to her lunch. "You sure were wigged out over something. I wish there had been something I could have done."

"You don't know how much you did do," she said in return. Jenna Rose froze in surprise at the sound of her own words. Wow, was she really admitting that?

Darby dropped her half-eaten piece of pizza to her plate and took a drink. "Sure didn't seem like anything to me."

"Believe me, it was. Thanks."

Darby knocked her with her elbow and smiled. "But you still aren't going to tell me what that was all about, are you?"

Jenna Rose shook her head sheepishly. "I don't know what there is to say. It's all really stupid."

"*Stupid* isn't quite the word I would use for the way you were acting the other day."

Jenna Rose concentrated on her sandwich.

No, I will not talk about it. It's already done and past.

"Let's just drop it, okay?" she found herself saying.

"Okay," Darby replied, rather taken aback. "But if you need to talk. . ."

"Yeah, yeah," Jenna Rose interrupted. "I get it." She dug once again in her bag and retrieved a bag of baby carrots. "So where are your sister and Shanice?"

"Making copies of the flyer. They were hoping to have at least some of them done before lunch was over. We can hand them out while they eat."

Hand them out? Uh, no.

"You know," Jenna Rose stated, glancing at the clock. "I need to get to the guidance counselor and drop that study hall. I was supposed to do that today." She was relieved to see that Darby was satisfied with her excuse. "But as soon as I'm done, I'll catch up with you." She tossed her things back in the bag as she spoke to look more convincing. Uneasily, she glanced at two girls at the table behind her as they whispered and giggled. Both were staring at Jenna Rose.

She scooped up her stuff, waved to Darby, and hurriedly dropped her trash in the waste bin. A third girl had joined the duo, and all three seemed to be watching her as they whispered.

Whatever their deal is, it probably has something to do with Jamie Valentin.

She snapped her thoughts back to the flyers. The promotional side of the band had never crossed her mind. Promoting the project meant people had to see her and connect her with Second Rate. *People,* including Jamie Valentin.

It wasn't that she was above handing out band flyers. She could hand out flyers all day—it was a great way to meet new people. It was just the fact that Jamie or any of his friends could come around and give her a hard time. Right now she was looking for ways to blend in—not stick out. At least until this stuff with him died out.

Collecting her stuff, she hurried out of the lunchroom and down the hall. The study hall had been taken care of days ago, but it was the first excuse that popped into her head. All she knew was that she was not handing out anything right now. She was just going to blend into the walls somewhere until her next class.

As she rounded the corner, she glanced at her watch, still trying to decide what she was going to do for the last fifteen minutes of lunch. She could head to the library and browse around for a bit or else step outside for some fresh spring air. If she wanted to trudge all the way upstairs, Mr.

Scott needed to see her about setting up those voice lessons.

Voice lessons. How funny. I could give voice lessons.

"Hi," someone stated. She looked up to see Jamie Valentin in his baseball jersey and a pair of breakaways standing in a doorway close to her locker. "Can we talk?"

Part of her wanted to turn and run. But her feet wouldn't move. She was tired of running. It was time to get this over with. "I really have nothing to say to you," she replied.

"Please," he begged, a sincerity coming through that she hadn't heard from him before. His eyes were rather charming when he wasn't being a stalker freak from a bad slasher movie.

Sheesh, woman, get a grip.

"I know you haven't read the notes I left you. You just threw them away," Jamie said. "I really need to talk to you."

She stopped and walked toward him. "Fine, but let's talk right here in the hall."

"Fair." He threw his hands up as he said the word. "Look, this has not gone the way it should have."

"What is it you are telling people about me, Jamie?" Suddenly, she felt like Jenna Rose Brinley again. Not this Ohio Jenna who was intimidated and awkward around guys, but the real Jenna Rose, the one who had guys eating out of her hand. The one she knew and loved. . .the one *everybody* knew and loved.

Again, he tossed up his hands. A twinkle in his eye confessed of his lie before he even spoke the words. "I had nothing to do with any rumors. Swear."

Crossing her arms in front of herself, she rocked slightly, unsure of his intentions.

"I would really like to make it up to you."

"What? If you had nothing to do with the rumors, what do you have to make up about?"

"Fair enough again. I don't know what it is, but I really can't stop thinking about you," he said sweetly, reaching out for her hand. She held her grip firmly on her books. "I really would like the chance to get to know you."

"Thanks but no thanks," she stated quietly and turned to walk away.

He reached out and grabbed her arm.

That same feeling of dread washed over her at his touch. His fingers were callused and dry and bit into her flesh as he pulled her closer to him again.

Placing his forehead against hers, he held tight to her arm and leaned into her as he spoke. His patience was wearing thin—she could hear it in his breath. "I am not a terrible guy."

"I never said you were," she replied, willing someone to walk around the corner.

Telepathy, if you are ever going to work, don't fail me now.

"Can you give me another chance?" He flashed a smile that told Jenna Rose he usually got his way. He really wasn't used to the way she was reacting to him. She squirmed again, but his grip was unrelenting.

"Look, let's play this straight. You're a hot new girl in school. You go out with me, and you won't be new for long. Everyone will know you."

Just what I wanted. . .but look where it got me.

Strangely enough, the idea of having popularity handed to her that easily wasn't tempting. She almost chuckled to herself at how quickly she brushed away the idea. No way was this going to be the price she paid for getting *in*.

Again the idea of screaming crossed her mind. What good was it really going to do? Would anyone actually hear her?

The murmur of voices soon answered her question. A group of people was heading toward them down the locker-lined corridor. A small cry escaped her lips as his grip dug farther into her arm. He wasn't letting go.

Amber and Shanice rounded the corner, stacks of the flyers filling their hands. Two skaters followed along behind them, surveying the paper. They chattered among themselves as they walked, oblivious at first to her presence.

Jamie slipped his arm around her waist, still holding onto her arm and smiling as the boys walked by. The smell of him was making her ill.

If ESP is ever going to work, make it now.

Jenna Rose looked longingly at her friends as they froze at the sight of her in his arms.

"Hey," Shanice stated in amazement.

Please, please get me out of this.

"Hey," Jamie replied in his popular I'm-a-star-baseball-player voice. He turned to Jenna Rose and asked as if he were excited to meet them, "Are these friends of yours?"

Jenna Rose nodded.

Tell him you need my help. Ask him why he's pinching the circulation out of my arm. Mention the fact that I have never once talked about him. Do something.

" 'Sup," he stated. "Whatcha got there?"

Don't show him. Don't tell him. Do not let him know.

"Flyers for our show Saturday night," Amber stated. "I'm sure Jenna Rose told you about it." Her tone was flat and laced with sarcasm.

What's that supposed to mean?

Letting go of her elbow, he reached for one of the papers. Jenna Rose flexed her arm as a dull pain rushed through it. Shanice was looking at her—she hoped Shanice had seen the marks left by his grip. Scrunching her lips together, Jenna Rose shifted her eyes down to her arm. The other girl didn't seem to notice.

What are you so afraid of? Just tell them. What can he do to you?

"You know," Jenna Rose proclaimed, taking the chance to get away from him, "I really should go help them get these out."

"Sure," he agreed, still in popular guy mode. "I'll catch you before the day's over."

Her heart jumped into her throat. "Sure," she whispered.

For good measure, she grabbed the stack of papers from Shanice's hands and hurried back around the corner. Amber followed behind her. Halfway back to the cafeteria, Shanice stopped. Her hair was still in the same braided pattern that it had been the night before at the photo shoot. Jenna Rose remained fascinated with the time commitment it must have taken to do it. Shanice's baggy khakis with the wide legs and her favorite "christian girl" T-shirt shifted to one side as she thrust a hip out and looked over Jenna Rose defiantly.

"What's up with you two?" she asked in full Shanice attitude, thumbing in Jamie's direction.

"Nothing," Jenna Rose stated, feeling like she was about to puke. The smell of him—the smell of fear—still hung in her nose.

"I thought you were crushing on Parker?"

I knew somebody had to know.

Jenna Rose's mouth fell open as she looked from Amber back to Shanice. Both sets of eyes were fixed intently on her. Waiting and wanting the big answer. These two weren't the stupid ones—they knew what she was doing in this group. "I was. I did. I mean, I am," she stumbled. "I like Parker."

Sure would have been a lot easier to say it a long time ago had I known you all had it figured out.

"I like all you guys," she added quickly, though her statement sounded fake even to her. "You're my only friends here."

Shanice looked at Amber and cocked her head. Smacking her lips loudly, she returned her gaze to Jenna Rose. "So which one you playing?"

"Wha. . . ?" She couldn't even finish the word as anger boiled up in her. "Are you serious?"

If you and Amber would have opened your eyes back there, maybe you would have a clue.

"Look, Jenna, Parker is one of my best friends, and if you are just here to play head games, keep movin', because I'm not going for it." As she spoke, she glanced at Amber, who seemed to just get smaller and smaller with each word.

"Shanice, I can assure you. . ."

"This group of friends here—this band," she continued, "they mean everything to us." She pointed her finger back at Amber and herself. "I

133

am not going to let you just walk in here and destroy it all."

"Who says. . ." As usual, she found herself tongue-tied. The words were there in her head but so jumbled she couldn't get them to come out coherently. Her face burned in hurt and embarrassment.

Shanice took a step closer and took the flyers back. "You are free to live your own life, Jenna Rose Brinley. But I am not going to let you tear apart this band before it even gets off the ground."

She spun around, a wave of braids cascading behind her, and headed back to the cafeteria.

Amber lingered for a moment, unsure of what to do. She watched Shanice walk away and then turned and stared at Jenna Rose again. This time, Jenna Rose understood the look in her eyes.

Mistrust.

CHAPTER 22

I f she were Amy or had just a little of her former confidence, she would have spilled the whole story. She would have told them the truth about Jamie Valentin. She would have told them about Parker being clueless about her feelings for him and how the whole scenario was driving her crazy. She would have just spouted it all off in eloquent, tear-jerking, movie-of-the-week climactic fashion, and they would have all hugged and been friends. Instead, she sat on the bus, alone, thinking about how she could have fixed the situation when it happened.

But she wasn't Amy. And she was really no more than a shell of her old and bold self.

"Hot tub," thug boy Jason reminded her as he strutted past her seat. She pretended she didn't hear him. If only she could melt away into the seats so the idiots couldn't see her.

Dogwood petals blew through the open bus window. Jenna Rose leaned her head against the cool glass and watched the dark storm clouds roll around in the distance. Drawing in a deep breath, she held it for as long as she could take. The scent of dogwoods and impending rain—smells so close to home—to Georgia—the first she had noticed since leaving there. Closing her eyes, the scent carried her back to a place where her best friend didn't yell at her and the guys she liked returned her feelings.

The bus lurched forward, bringing her out of her daydream. The seat beside her was empty. She viewed her surroundings and saw Parker was nowhere in sight. Just perfect. Of all the days she could use his shoulder for support, he was nowhere to be seen.

At home she found that her dad was gone as usual—with no note telling of his whereabouts. Flipping through the mail, she walked through their house, the smell of old wallpaper and Pine-Sol still lingering in the air. She should burn some candles to get rid of it. This house could never really have a chance of being their home if it still smelled like someone else's cleaning supplies. *As if this house even has a chance of being my home.*

She dropped the mail on his desk and grabbed her favorite glass—a molded glass freebie from an old fast-food movie-promotion tie-in. Opting for the whole bag of cookies rather than a few, she headed to the backyard. Carson wasn't on TRL anymore anyway. Besides, a warm spring day beat out music videos and annoying model-perfect audience interviews.

Jenna Rose sat on the back step and opened her bag of cookies. She had an hour until their last rehearsal before the big gig. Plenty of time to drown in milk-drenched cookie-goo and decide if she should really show up or not. Things were definitely not going her way so far—first her dad ditched her on the cookie tradition, and now Carson wasn't even on. . . .

"We must have moved into the house everyone shunned," she mused. All three backyards connected to theirs were fenced in—with chain link on the left, an eight-foot-high wood fence stretching across the back, and cute white picket border on the right. It gave her yard the illusion of being protected in a mix-matched kind of way.

I could have sworn we had our own fence when we moved in here.

A barren, weed-strewn backyard filled the fenced-in space. . .pretty sad. Jenna Rose felt a bit of pity for it. She knew what it was like to look put together when the reality was just an empty, mixed-up mess.

She could probably fix this place up. Maybe plant a dogwood, or a rosebush, or both. If she could get some chairs and a bird feeder, it could be pretty homey. They could even get a grill and maybe one of those patio tables with an umbrella. It would be a few years before the dogwood would be able to shade them while they ate. It could even become her favorite space.

The whirl of skateboard wheels spinning across the asphalt driveway jolted her out of her planning.

Great.

It was one of them. Who else could it be? It wasn't just one of them—it had to be Parker.

The sound stopped, and then she heard the doorbell ring. Her heart racing, she sat very still, trying to decide what she should do. Was he coming to yell at her some more like Shanice did? Or maybe to tell her to leave him alone?

But what if he was coming to express his feelings for her?

What then?

She couldn't bring herself to move. Why was he here? Jenna Rose knew there were rumors being spread about her by Jamie, and she knew how the system worked. Simple deduction based on the sudden interest of Hot Tub Boy and other creeps showed what kind of stories he was telling—false ones about what really happened between them in the vending machine room at school.

Parker had shown her no real interest until the rumors started to fly.

Then he appeared around the corner. He carried the board in his hand as it bounced against his baggy cutoff green shorts. The black Christian band T-shirt was more fitted than most of the shirts he wore and really showed off his lanky physique.

"Hi," he stated. Then his eyes followed her gaze to his legs. "Oh, don't look at those. They'll glow in the dark."

Like always, he set her at ease immediately. Whatever he was here for, it was going to be all right.

"May I?" he asked, pointing to the stoop beside her.

She scooted over to the edge, arranging her cookie bag and cup to make room for him.

He's going to think I'm a pig sitting with a whole bag of cookies.

Putting one foot on his board, he took a seat beside her and stared out into the backyard. She pictured what the perfectly manicured lawn behind his cute little ranch house must look like and felt embarrassed that he had to see this mess.

"So," she stated, desperate to hear something other than the silence between them. Silence was a bad sign. Silence meant "I don't know what I'm going to say yet so I need to think about it for a bit." No one comes to visit unannounced not knowing what to say if they have good news.

"You excited about tomorrow night?" he finally asked. "Our first big gig."

She sighed, fighting off the urge to shove a whole cookie in her mouth. Pigs can't talk and explain things. She so needed to be a pig right now.

"Parker, I don't know about tomorrow night."

"What?" He slid his hands through his hair and turned his attention back to the trio of fences. "You nervous?"

"No, I don't think it's a good idea that I be there," she replied.

Again, he ran his fingers through his hair. "Why not?"

Jenna Rose wished that he would look at her. Instead, he continued to stare at the dirt mound near the chain link fence. If only she could read his mind. . .then she would know exactly how much he knew and what she didn't have to say.

"I just don't think it would be a good idea."

"Jenna, what's going on? You don't have to hide everything inside, you know? You do have friends. Talk to me."

Yeah, like the two "friends" who attacked me today? Sure I do.

She smirked and replied sourly, "I don't know who my friends are around here."

"If you'd give people a chance, you would find out."

Sure, but when is someone going to give me a chance?

She shook her head, once again afraid to say the words that were right there ready to come forth. The right words always got stuck, while the things she shouldn't say slipped through.

Again they sat in silence. Birds fluttered and chirped all around them, skipping over her desolate yard for the decadent treats waiting in those fancy fenced-in yards.

Everyone skips over me now, even the birds.

"Why don't you like me?" The words came out before she knew they had formed on her tongue. She tried to suck them back in as they escaped, but it was too late.

Parker ran his fingers through his curls—curls she would never get to caress—and scratched the back of his neck. "Jenna Rose," he whispered.

Have you ever called me by my full name? Great.

"No, never mind. I'm sorry I even asked it." She stopped him before he could say any more. Biting her quivering lip, she fought back the tears that stung at her eyes.

She didn't want to know. Panicked, she swiped up her cookies and stood up, but there was no place to go—her messed up, mixed-up yard was all blocked in by other people's fences, and he was crowding the door so she couldn't go inside. She was trapped.

He reached out and gingerly took her hand in his. Her knees almost buckled.

I will not be weak.

"I am so sorry," he began. "I've never meant for you to think that I didn't like you."

There had to be a "but." There was always a "but."

She stood awkwardly as he held her hand. She stared out at the tall fence, unable to look at Parker. She wondered what was so special behind that fence that it was all protected like that so you couldn't see in.

Yeah, that's it. Think about anything but what's going on right now.

"What's wrong with us this way?" He dropped her hand and sighed at his own statement. "Wait. Let me try to explain. I'm not like you, Jenna. I didn't grow up in a strong Christian home knowing who Christ was from the day I was born."

Turning to look at him, she readjusted her fingers in his grip. Oh, but if he only knew what he was talking about. Like her life was so cut-and-dry perfect.

"See, Darby talked me into going to a concert last summer. If I had known it was a religious thing, I would have come up with every excuse in the book not to go. We were taking guitar lessons together, and I thought she had to be the coolest chick I'd ever seen. I was willing to go just about anywhere to be around her."

The lump in her throat returned.

So there's some truth to the "Parker and I" stuff.

"I went to this Christian concert," Parker continued, thrusting his hands into his pockets. His gaze was firmly planted on his shoes as he twitched anxiously back and forth. "And I was so blown away, Jenna. I've never felt more alive in all my life. Never."

Jenna Rose knew that feeling. She had left many concerts and rallies in her day feeling so on fire and ready to light up the world with what she was feeling. The funny thing was it usually fizzled for her before they made it home.

He lifted his eyes and caught her gaze with his. "You see, I haven't known Christ for a whole year yet. I made a promise to Him and to myself that I needed time to get to know Him. It's not that I don't like you, Jenna. Man, I thought you'd have seen it a hundred times by now. It has nothing to do with you. I thought you knew I was crazy about you."

The tears started to stream down her face. Silently, she begged herself to understand what he was talking about. She wasn't sure that she could.

His eyes were so gorgeous. She couldn't stand to look at them any longer. As a bird flew by, she turned her attention to the ground where it came from.

Stupid, stupid. You weren't supposed to let him see you cry.

"But I can't date you right now," he stated, tugging on her arm gently so she would lift her head. "I'm not dating anyone. And I'm not planning to date anyone. The Bible says He has someone intended for each of us, and when His timing is right, He'll reveal it, right?"

She nodded. If she had a nickel for every time she had heard that sentiment from her dad. . .

"Well, I'm not going to risk messing up His plan," Parker stated confidently.

"But I don't get it. You think God told you not to date?" She choked out the words, determined that she was not going to end up a blubbering fool in his presence.

"I think God told me that the easiest way to keep myself pure is not to date. I made mistakes before. I know the road dating can lead to, and I feel the best way to keep myself from going that way again is to focus on one relationship right now: my relationship with Christ. If my faith were as strong as yours is, I might think differently. I might be able to act differently, but right now I'm not at that point."

Now she felt stupid. She had thrown herself at him over and over again, and yet he still saw her as this perfect Christian preacher's daughter. If only he knew the truth!

"Please don't leave the band on my account. We need you too much. I don't want to be the cause of you not being a part of it," he said. "I like things the way they are now between us. What's so wrong with that?"

"It's not that," she whispered, barely able to talk. He pulled her back down to her seat and laid his arm loosely around her shoulder. She felt so safe and good there as she snuggled down into his shoulder. Her tears started to come faster.

"Do you think I think the rumors are true?"

She gasped as she shook her head. So there really were rumors. And he really did know about them.

"I don't really care what you think," she lied in defense.

"I think you do or you wouldn't be sitting here right now."

"Well, I don't," she shot back, lifting her head up off his shoulder. She pulled away from him and stood up.

"Okay," he replied. After a moment's silence, he added, "We all make mistakes, Jenna Rose."

A mistake?

So you think I did it? You believe Jamie Valentin and his rumor mill over me?

"Yeah, I can see that," she stated firmly, jumping up. "I think I've made a big one." She grabbed the door handle and shoveled him off the step as she opened the screen door.

"Wait a minute," he pleaded as she slammed the inside door. "Jenna, please! Maybe that didn't come out the way it should have. I have made so many mistakes. If you knew how many times I've messed up like that in the past, you would know that I would be the last one here condemning you for what happened between you and Jamie Valentin."

"Go away, Parker," she shouted through the door.

He continued, "Just let me finish, please. Maybe I made the mistake."

"Maybe? No, believe me, I have. Now go away. I thought you were the one person that would hear them and just know that they weren't true. If there was one person in this school that I thought even slightly knew me, I thought it was you. I guess I was wrong."

"I don't believe the rumors, Jenna."

"Yeah, right. Obviously you do or we wouldn't be having this conversation right now. Go away before I call my dad and have him remove you." She locked the door as noisily as possible just for added effect. She had no idea where to even look for her dad—he could be at the church, a nursing home, the hospital, someone's house. Who knew?

"I said I don't believe the rumors," he called out again. "I really don't. I never really did. I just wanted to make sure that you were okay. Something had to have happened to give him that kind of ammo to say something like that. I just wanted to make sure you were okay."

But she didn't believe him.

Maybe it didn't even matter. There wasn't going to be a Jenna-and-Parker, so what did it matter what he thought?

Through the window in the door, she watched him pick up his board and walk down the drive. Something in her heart told her if she could just make herself run to him, everything would be all right between them. But she knew it wouldn't.

So what if I came on to Jamie. Or maybe I did flirt too much. Still, I never would have thought Parker could believe the nasty rumors flying around.

If only one person could have believed the truth, she had been sure it would be Parker.

She was wrong.

J enna Rose awoke with a start at the sound of the phone ringing. It had been a fitful night of sleep. No amount of exhaustion could overcome the thoughts zipping through her mind as she had tried to fall asleep, but at some point in time, fatigue had gotten the best of her. She had drifted off with her feet on her pillow and her comforter wrapped around her head.

"Honey," her dad called up the stairs. She could hear the bustle of his Saturday morning churchies in the background.

Those kids better not be eating my cookies and jumping on my couch.

"It's for you."

She pounced from bed, sure of who was calling. Since moving to Ohio, she had received only enough phone calls to count on one hand. With no pending appointments to remind her about, she knew this had to be Amy.

She grabbed her phone. "I got it," she told him, sure that she heard the sound of preschoolers munching on her cookies in the background.

"Okay, honey," he replied into the phone. "Good luck tonight, Darby."

Tricked.

She could hang up the phone. But that wouldn't be fair to Darby— the tall twin had done nothing wrong.

"Hello," Jenna Rose muttered.

"Hi," came the reply. "Missed you last night."

"I'm sure you know why I wasn't there."

143

After a few seconds of hesitation, she replied, "Yeah, and I can't say that I blame you."

"Really?" Jenna Rose voiced her surprise.

"Well, yeah. I think it's pretty shady that Shanice went flying off the handle like that without at least getting your side of the story."

Wow.

"So what do you think?" Jenna Rose prodded.

"Well, I know for a fact the rumor about Mr. Scott isn't true."

"Wait a minute," Jenna Rose blurted out, almost dropping the phone. She flopped dramatically back on the bed. "What about Mr. Scott? The band director Mr. Scott?"

"Yeah. There's a story going around that you skipped class to," Darby stammered a bit, looking for the right words to say, "be with Mr. Scott."

"People believe this? The band director?" she shrieked in surprise.

Mullet Boy. I could rip the hair right off the back of his neck.

"I don't know. When I heard about it, I backed you up. I said I was there the whole time, and it wasn't anything like that."

"Thanks," she mumbled, flabbergasted. Of all the rumors, she never would have imagined one about her and a teacher.

"Well, then when I heard about the other rumors about Jamie Valentin and Matt Schmidt, I kind of put two and two together."

"Who's Matt Schmidt?"

"One of Jamie's buddies, another baseball player, kind of got a mulletlike thing going on."

"Okay, I know who you're talking about. I've never even spoken to him. He was the one stalking me that day I flipped out on you in the bathroom," Jenna Rose found herself explaining. She told Darby all about the day of dance team tryouts and how she had flirted with Jamie just for something fun to do. She told her about his following her in the halls, the letters, the school bus, and the confrontation with Shanice.

She stopped herself short before talking about yesterday's conversation with Parker. He had disappointed her, and she didn't want to recall it, much less share it with someone whom he held dear. Besides, it was just difficult to think about him right now.

The heavy beating of her heart seemed to echo through the room as she waited for Darby to say something. As long as the girl didn't tell her she deserved it, Jenna Rose would be fine. She could deal with it.

"Jenna," Darby said finally, "if you would have told somebody, this wouldn't have all had to happen."

"Darby, please. Who's honestly going to believe the new girl in school over the star jock who's plastered all over the news? Plus. . ." she tapered off, not sure if she could bring herself to say it.

"You could have told one of us," came the reply.

She closed her eyes as she said the words. "I know you had to have noticed how I was trying to pick up Parker."

Darby laughed, setting Jenna Rose's mind at ease. "We may be an odd bunch, but we're not blind. We picked up on that a few times."

"Hard not to, I guess," Jenna Rose added, poking fun at herself.

"Jenna Rose, please say you're coming tonight."

"I don't think so," she replied. "I don't think the band wants me there. I don't think Parker even wants me there after the way I treated him last night."

"Second Rate is just as much a part of you as it is any of the rest of us. You put in just as much work. Shoot, you let my sister dress you!"

"I don't know, Darby."

"Look, I have to get going. We're heading down to the church to set up. We need you. Not just because you have that killer voice. We need you because you are one of us. So you had a little fight with Shanice. Get used to it. That's how she is. But she's quick to forgive and forget and move on. Honest. Please?"

"I'd think she'd rather me not be there so she can sing."

"Nah, she really wants what's best for the band. We all know that's the two of you singing together. I'll see you in a bit, okay?"

"I just don't know," Jenna Rose replied before she hung the phone up. Making things right with Shanice was not going to be the hard part.

Jenna Rose fixated on her watch again, feeling very much like she did the first time she went to the pizza shop alone to meet up with the band. Intruding. That's what she felt like she was doing. Sneaking into a place where she didn't belong and where she wasn't completely wanted.

Even in the churches her father had pastored, she felt like an outsider looking in through the stained glass windows. Being in this big, beautiful church, she was sure the word "hypocrite" must be branded across her forehead for the whole world to see. She had no business singing lead for a Christian band. The lyrics that she sang were little more than words to her. They had to know.

That's what she came to do.

She would tell her friends the truth. With any luck, she might salvage a friendship or two after this charade was through. She was not the perfect Christian. She was not the perfect anything. And Shanice was right. She had no business tearing down the band before they even got it together.

They deserved an explanation—at least Parker and Darby did. Hopefully they could still find a way to be her friends.

The irony in it all was too amusing. She was about to beg for their forgiveness, even though she had been trying to avoid their attention at all costs not long before. Jenna Rose had tried very hard to distance herself from this group of teens, but in the meantime, somehow, she had become one of them.

Now she just had to figure out how to keep her place among them in some form.

She stood in the back of the fellowship hall. The room was packed around her. The crowd size was impressive for a high school garage band's opening gig. The main lights were off and a set of spotlights that must have belonged to the church was dancing around on the stage. A smile crossed her face as she watched Parker play his guitar, his eyes sweeping the crowd. Unlike Darby, who was perched on a barstool watching her fingers, he played with the crowd as his music flowed. Darby seemed to enter her own world where it was just her and her guitar.

They really started without me. I was right. They didn't need me at all.

With a sigh, she realized that she had left them little choice, holed up in her room not answering the phone. Really, what were they supposed to do? They couldn't leave all these people hanging on their first gig.

Shanice stood somewhat timidly behind the microphone stand, her arms at her sides as she began to sing. A large silver cross hung from the purple-carpeted wall behind her. If they could stay friends, Jenna Rose would need to work with her on her stage presence. A lead singer has no business looking like she is trying to use a mike stand as a shield. Shanice needed more than a voice—she needed poise and command. If she were willing, Jenna Rose could help her fix that.

She knew Second Rate could go on without her, but it didn't make it any easier to watch.

They were about to finish the second song in the set. That meant Andria was going to speak for a moment before they would start on their third and last song before the intermission. During intermission she would find them and beg for their forgiveness for her deceit. She would let them know that she had no business being part of their group and that she had no hard feelings toward anyone.

She only hoped they would do the same for her.

As the crowd swayed and sang along with the popular worship tune, Jenna Rose realized she had to get closer to the stage. There was no possible way for her to stay in her safety net in the back and still get there in time to catch up with them before they broke for intermission.

Just please don't any of you guys see me.

That would just be too awkward for all of them. Plus, it just wouldn't be fair to interrupt them like this on their big night. They were probably going to be pretty mad at her—for her timing if nothing else. Hindsight was screaming at her that she should have done this *before* they went on stage.

"Jenna!" she heard a slightly familiar voice call. Scanning the crowd, she saw no friendly face to go with it. Maybe it wasn't meant for her. "Jenna Rose!"

It was for her.

The McKennitt twins' cousin pushed his way through the crowd, his camera in hand. What was his name?

Chance. Just perfect.

"What's goin' on?" he yelled, leaning close to her to hear over the music. "Why aren't you on stage?"

"Long story," she replied.

Behind him, a group of three guys who closely resembled Mullet Boy, Jamie, and another guy in a baseball team T-shirt made their way into the crowd from the door. Jenna Rose slumped down quickly behind Chance. She couldn't believe he was there. The trio went past and headed for the front of the stage. What was he going to do when he saw she wasn't singing?

"But, you're like the lead singer," Chance stated, still confused. "You want me to help you get up to the front?"

"I don't think they want me up there," she yelled over the band, staying close to him and out of sight.

Chance laughed. "Are you kidding? They were going nuts trying to find you earlier."

"They were?" Jenna Rose's eyebrows knitted together. After talking to Darby that morning, Jenna Rose had spent her afternoon on the computer, studying landscaping plans for her backyard and wallowing in self-pity over the way things had fallen into one big, messy heap instead of turning out the way they should have. She should be Parker's girlfriend, and she should be singing lead in this band that everyone around her was really into at the moment.

"Come on. Let's get you up there."

"I really don't think I should be." Her eyes darted about, watching for Jamie to reappear.

"Why not?" Chance yelled.

"I'm in no shape to be in a Christian band. I'm fake, Chance, compared to all of them. I don't have faith like them. I'd just ruin the whole thing."

Chance placed his hand on her elbow and led her around the corner into the hallway. "It's quieter out here. I couldn't hear you. Say that again?"

Jenna Rose repeated herself, looking very small. The words had been much less daunting to say in the dark, loud room where the band was playing.

"If we were perfect, Jenna," he stated, his voice still raised to be heard above the music, "there would have been no reason for Christ. There isn't a perfect Christian out there, and if you find someone that says he is, I doubt he's really a Christian."

"I don't know, Chance. I made a big mistake doing this. I don't belong up there." She exhaled deeply, searching for the words that might make some sense. "Maybe once I become a better person again—"

He cut her off. "Ah, but that's just it. You can't become anything on your own. If you're looking to find perfection in yourself by your own doing, it's not going to happen. The only way there is ever going to be perfection in you is through Jesus Christ."

Jenna Rose laid her head back against the corkboard bulletin board on the wall.

If only it were that easy.

Shanice's sultry voice rang out. "I could sing of your love forever." Jenna Rose believed Shanice probably could. But she couldn't. How could she sing something like that when she wasn't even sure if she believed that He existed? How could she do the band justice—the music justice—if she wasn't even sure she believed in whom she was singing about? Her feet slid as she scooted down the wall into a sitting position, wrapping her arms around her knees and drawing them close to her. Chance sat down next to her.

"Everyone's always just assumed you know Christ and have a real relationship with Him, haven't they?" Chance asked.

He had beautiful hazel almond-shaped eyes and the kind of lashes most girls would envy. They were gentle yet playful eyes with a sparkle that reminded her of Parker's. That something special in Parker that she couldn't quite pinpoint was there in Chance too.

"Of course," she replied. "I'm the preacher's kid, you know? If anyone has to have it all together, that would be me."

"What's stopping you then?" he nudged gently. The words would have been harsh coming from anyone else's mouth.

"I don't know. Life. And you don't have to give me reasons to believe and all. I know all about the plan of salvation. I could recite the Scripture for you if you want to hear it. I've heard them all and I even understand it, but I'm just not sure for myself."

"I guess that's where faith steps in."

"Yeah, I guess," she mumbled shortly.

Shanice finished the song and Andria began talking. Jenna Rose got to her feet and went back inside the room. Andria stood barefoot next to her sister with a mike clutched in her hand. She was saying something about gifts and talents and using them as God intended, but Jenna Rose no longer was able to hear her.

Jamie Valentin stood squarely in front of Jenna Rose, his hands thrust deep into his pockets. A smug, wry grin covered his face.

CHAPTER 25

Jenna Rose backed up against the doorframe, silently praying that Chance was still right on the other side. If only he could witness anything that happened with this psycho. Maybe then all the trouble would stop.

"Why aren't you on stage?" Jamie asked. "I came to watch you sing."

Jenna Rose shrugged her shoulders. She owed him no explanations. *Please, please, don't go anywhere, Chance.*

"I thought we had a date tonight."

"You said we had a date," she replied. "I never agreed to it. And I'm not going to go anywhere with you."

Shaking his head slowly, he laughed. "You really are something, aren't you?" Jamie sneered as Chance stepped around the corner. "Who's this? You with older guys now?"

Chance stepped between Jenna Rose and Jamie. "I think it's time for you to just step back."

The baseball player lifted his head, showing fire burning in his eyes, and his arms flexed. "I don't know who you are, but this doesn't involve you. So, I think *you* need to just step back."

Andria announced from the stage that the band was taking a short break. Straining to see which direction her friends went, Jenna Rose stretched to see over the crowd. She couldn't believe Jamie's timing. Why did this Neanderthal have to be here and make even more of a

151

mess of this whole thing?

"You know, Jamie, get it through your thick, stupid head that nothing happened between you and me. And nothing is *ever* going to happen between you and me."

She wasn't sure where she mustered the strength to say it, but relief washed over her as she did.

Darby was the last band member to disappear into the crowd. She couldn't see any of them anywhere.

"I don't understand why you're doing this to me," he stated, suddenly changing his tone to a victimized whine. "I really thought we could have something real."

Chance spun to look at her, questioning in his eyes. She flared her nostrils and rolled her eyes. It really was hopeless.

Turning back to Jamie, Chance said, "No, I don't know what's going on here, but you are obviously making my friend uncomfortable. I need to ask you to walk away, or I'll see that you're escorted out."

At that moment Jenna Rose heard a squeal. Darby broke through the crowd and scooped Jenna Rose into her arms. "You did make it!"

The rest of the group broke through the crowd around her. Parker, standing with his arms crossed in front of him, appeared next to Jamie. Jenna Rose was afraid to look at any of the band—her eyes stared straight at the boy who had caused her so much grief and pain. This was ending. One way or another, it was all ending now.

Mullet Boy returned to the scene with a soda in hand. He took one look at Jenna Rose and laughed. "Hi there, sweetheart. Look at you." He scanned her outfit, letting his eyes purposely hover over the Transformer print on her fitted T-shirt. A chill ran up her spine as she refrained from shrinking back from his sight.

"Couldn't cut the dance team, so she decided to become a freak," replied Jamie, his voice dripping in sarcasm. They high-fived.

A small crowd started to gather, curious to know if the confrontation was real or a staged group of friends. Many people streamed past, making their way to the concession stand.

Someone had put a CD on to play through intermission. The song, a familiar tune that her dad played often, fueled Jenna Rose's adrenaline. She was not running this time. She was not hiding.

"What you've been saying about me isn't true," she stated firmly, moving past Chance and facing Jamie directly, "and it needs to stop now."

"All I did was tell a couple of friends," Jamie replied, making a dismissive sweep of his hand. "You know how these things take on a life of their own. It's too bad about the rumors and all, but you and I both know what happened last weekend. What's wrong? Don't want to admit it in front of all your church friends here and all, huh?" he sneered.

"You need to leave," Chance responded again. "Now."

Jenna Rose placed a hand on Chance's chest, her eyes not leaving Jamie. "I got this, Chance. I'm not playing these games with him anymore." Respecting her decision, the college senior stepped back, his eyes also not leaving Jamie.

"I'm tired of this, Jamie. I don't care who you are. I'm not interested in you, and I'm not going to put up with this drama from you any longer."

"What drama? You're acting like I'm stalking you or something. I tried to talk to you all week, and you got freaky on me. I just came here tonight to see this really nice girl I met last weekend perform, and you weren't even on stage. Why is that? You got something to be ashamed of or what?" Jamie laughed, shuffling his feet to look over the crowd that had gathered. Most of the faces were people he probably knew.

Jenna Rose also looked around. Save the band and her two assailants, there were no other faces even remotely familiar to her.

"Do you think people are going to believe you?" Jamie added.

"I do," Parker stated loudly.

Jenna Rose snapped her head toward him, astounded that he would stand up for her.

"Me too," Andria added, walking over beside Jenna Rose.

Oh, I wouldn't mess with that one, Jamie. She'll end up drop-kickin' you in the head or something.

Darby spoke up next. "I do."

"Same with me," Elijah also called from the crowd behind Jenna Rose. He pushed his way through the audience and stood beside Parker. With a quick smile at her, he crossed his arms like Parker, signaling his stance with his band mates.

"So do I," Amber stated confidently, "so do I."

Jenna Rose's chest pounded with a mixture of adrenaline and happiness. She felt like dancing in joy and puking at the same time. In part, she wanted to scan the crowd and look for Shanice. Maybe she wasn't in earshot and didn't know what was going on. Or maybe she was and didn't believe what Jenna Rose was saying. Not wanting to take her eyes off the jocks, Jenna Rose listened for her voice.

"I am so sorry I ever didn't," said Shanice as she came up behind her and touched Jenna Rose's arm slightly.

"You need to leave, Jamie," Parker added. "Unless you're here to sing some praises, you need to go."

Jamie shook his head and stuck his hands back in his pockets. "Choosing the freaks, are we, Jenna?"

Jenna Rose stared at him without flinching. Her back was soaked with perspiration, and she felt dizzy. This needed to end soon or she was going to pass out, and if Jamie Valentin saw the slightest bit of weakness in her, it would all start back up Monday morning at school. She could sweat off ten pounds before she budged. She smiled slightly at Parker, and he winked in return. Her knees felt like rubber.

Studying her face for a moment, Jamie nearly spat. "Well, amen, sister! Praise Juh-ee-zuz!" he shouted, heading to the door. "Don't think you'll have another turn."

CHAPTER 26

Okay, *this is awkward.*

Jenna Rose viewed the crowd again, purposely avoiding the eyes of those who had spoken out for her. She was still in awe that they had done that, and she didn't know what to say. The waterworks would probably start as soon as she made eye contact with one of them, so she just tried to keep from looking at any of them.

Sink into the floor, she tried to will herself. *Sink into the floor.*

Of course, she just stood there. Too bad all those cool things people could do in the movies weren't real.

Eventually I have to face them if I want to tell them the truth.

She still had to explain herself. She really wanted to tell them why she couldn't be in their band and apologize for ditching them.

"We need to get back on stage," Andria said. She seized Jenna Rose's arm and headed back into the crowd.

"Andria, I can't," Jenna Rose pleaded.

Second Rate's drummer held fast, weaving through the people congregating again in front of the stage. Shanice had a hand on Jenna Rose's back, and the others followed.

Again, Jenna Rose tried to tell them, but Andria held a finger to her lips as she pulled Jenna Rose onto the stage behind her. "We'll have time to talk later. We got a show to do."

She stumbled a bit as she made her way around the stage. Shanice bounced up beside her, pulling a second mike free and handing it to her. She grinned and whispered, "Welcome back."

As Darby started a melody on her guitar, Parker situated his instrument and stepped in front of the microphone. "Hey, hey, hey, guys," he addressed the crowd. "God's done such amazing stuff in my life in the past year. This time last year, man, I was so lost. I didn't think I was ever going to be found."

Jenna Rose stared at her feet as he spoke.

What am I doing? Get down from here now.

"When I first heard about this Jesus—" A group of guys in the audience began to cheer. "Yeah, you heard of that guy?" Parker asked, pointing to them with a chuckle. "I was like, cuz, I am so far away from that, from what you say He wants from me. You know, I was like, it's gonna take me forever to get there. You know, before I can even get to know Him, I got miles to go to get to a place where God would be. He wouldn't be in this messed-up thing I call life."

Jenna Rose snorted as she tried not to laugh. Laughing would not be a wise choice. She knew very well what he was talking about!

Shanice walked over beside her and put her arm around her shoulder. "The set list got changed just a bit," she whispered. "Parker's gonna sing one, and then we'll go straight into 'Above All.'"

Parker can sing?

Could the guy be any more perfect? She nodded in understanding.

"But you know the amazing thing?" Parker asked, slipping the microphone from its stand. He walked toward the two girls on the opposite side of the stage. "The coolest, greatest thing about my God? When I finally decided to take that long trek back, when I decided to turn around and go back through all that crud to get to Him, He was right there." Stopping beside Jenna Rose, he held up his palm toward his face as he said the last word.

Jenna Rose couldn't bring herself to look at him. After their fight the other day and the way she had slammed the door in his face, she never thought things could ever be the way they were before. She really showed her flawed, ugly self quickly that day. Yet at his words, *He was right there*, she had to look into his face. There was no way he could have known what she and Chance had been speaking about earlier. She had never said anything like that to Parker before. She'd never said anything like that to anyone—except Chance, and there hadn't been time for him to tell anyone else.

Darby's guitar part picked up just a bit as he finished.

Wow. She looked out at the crowd. There were so many faces. So many people to listen to not only their music and voices but their hearts and souls bared as well.

This is why I can't do this. These people are here to hear us bring our own stories of being close to God, and here I don't even know if He's real.

This time her feet had to work. Not so much for her sake, but for theirs—for the rest of Second Rate. As she contemplated where to put the microphone, Parker began to sing. She found herself nearly crumpling to the floor in tears.

She knew the song well—a song from a few years before that her father played often. Her dad loved that CD, and she secretly did too.

"I've heard it said that a man would climb a mountain," Parker sang, his voice rich and strong, "just to be with the one that he loves." She knew these words inside and out, but she had never really heard them until this moment.

The words came from Parker but the meaning came from somewhere else—from inside her heart and all around the room at the same time. Her knees felt weak as she put a hand to her mouth to try to calm herself.

Someone in the crowd started to sing, and more and more began to join in.

"Just to be with you I'd do anything. . . ," the room continued together. She was about to go down under the weight of the words. She was going down.

Parker reached out and took her hand. Once upon a time, she daydreamed about the moment he would hold his hand out, singing words such as these. Yet this time it was so much more than Parker

Blevins reaching for her with outstretched hands. Sobbing openly, she crumpled into his arms.

But what was this?

The insecurity, the fear, and even the doubt seemed to be no more. As she cried tears of joy in his arms, she didn't think she would ever know how those things felt again.

She had sought the love of the young man who embraced her and instead found a love that would move heaven and earth just to be with her.

Parker wrapped his arms tight around her as the crowd continued to sing in his place. It was a perfect embrace. Yet it didn't feel like the embrace was even coming from Parker Blevins's arms! Though Parker was holding her, the God he was so in love with was also there. She finally understood why the people whom she shared the stage with were impacting her so greatly—God had brought them all together.

God was real. Just like her mom had always said, He was real and He was right there with them. She opened her eyes to see the others—all except Darby still perched on her barstool, guitar in hand—circled around her. She smiled meekly at Andria as she squeezed her hand. Her friends.

She came to Ohio thinking she had lost everything. . .that her life was over. Any new life would never compare to what she had before—a best friend, popularity, and the attention of any guy she wanted. She'd thought she had everything in life, but now she knew she didn't have nearly enough.

Instead, she came to Ohio and gained the world.

"You okay?" Parker whispered as she dabbed at her eyes, still standing in his hug.

"Perfect," she replied.

"Can you go on?" he asked.

Jenna Rose smiled up at him, knowing that she was all right. Things weren't ever going to be the same between them again. She had a feeling that things were going to be better than she had ever imagined. As the song trailed off and the crowd began to cheer, Jenna Rose lowered her head and prayed for the first real time in her life.

God, I know I have heard this a thousand times in my life and never believed it for myself, but this time I know it's real. I know You are real. Please come into my life, Lord.

She held tightly to Parker's hand and grasped the microphone in the other.

My makeup is probably a wreck now.

She tossed the thought as quickly as it appeared. Like it really mattered!

Shanice was looking at her and smiling widely. Andria, drumsticks in hand, was poised and ready for her signal. Elijah's head bopped to the beat already going in his head, and Darby even looked up from her guitar as the crowd's cheers died down. Jenna Rose couldn't see Amber through the crowd, but she knew her other friend was ready and manning the soundboard, waiting for the signal.

Her friends. Her band. And they were waiting for her cue.

Jenna Rose smiled again and squeezed Parker's hand. "Second Rate, let's do it!"

Also in the On Tour Series

the backup singer

Sassy former lead-singer Shanice Stevenson is content with her role, backing up the gifted Jenna Rose, in the band's exciting new dynamic. That is, until a visit from her troubled cousin, raises questions of race and asks—what is the color of friendship?

From *The Backup Singer. . .*

"Are you even black?"

Shanice Stevenson dragged her heel on the sidewalk, bringing her in-line skates to a halt. With a flick of her ankles, she spun herself around to face the girl that had spoken to her with such malice.

The two teenaged boys accompanying her also skidded to a stop and turned toward the unfamiliar voice.

Elijah Greer, the taller of the two boys, skated over and took his friend by the arm. "Come on, 'Nice," he said gingerly, using her pet name and trying to diffuse the situation. "We aren't looking for any trouble. Let's skate."

The newcomer stood in the middle of the sidewalk, hands perched on her hips. Her eyes were fixed steadily on Shanice, challenging her to give an answer. The girl appeared to be in her mid-teens like the trio before her, but she wasn't a familiar face in their tight-knit neighborhood.

Chill, 'Nice, chill. Don't be stupid and don't give her the satisfaction. Just get away from her. Yeah, easier said than done.

Now Available in Bookstores

For more info about the band, sneak peeks of upcoming books, notes from the author, and more, check out www.ontourfanclub.com!